By Marek Moran

The Sparky

Published by Dreamspinner Press
www.dreamspinnerpress.com

THE SPARKY

Marek Moran

Published by
DREAMSPINNER PRESS

5032 Capital Circle SW, Suite 2, PMB# 279, Tallahassee, FL 32305-7886 USA
www.dreamspinnerpress.com

The Sparky
© 2017 Marek Moran.

Cover Art
© 2017 Catt Ford.
Cover content is for illustrative purposes only and any person depicted on the cover is a model.

ISBN: 978-1-63533-446-3
Digital ISBN: 978-1-63533-447-0
Library of Congress Control Number: 2016917542
Published March 2017
v. 1.0

Printed in the United States of America

This paper meets the requirements of
ANSI/NISO Z39.48-1992 (Permanence of Paper).

CHAPTER 1

THE TAXI'S nearing the house when I get a text. It has a +1 country code: Xavier. He must have worked out when I'd arrive, which is pretty thoughtful. *Hope the flight was OK. Missing you*, it says. Yeah, definitely thoughtful; it brings on a smile.

But I have to shove my phone away and get my wallet out because we've stopped. The driver's tapping on the wheel—the trip home already gave me a hint about his lack of patience, slaloming between cars on the major roads and ski-jumping over speed humps on the minor ones—and I just want to get out and into my house anyway. He honks—I look up, see a removalist truck that appears to have been mostly unpacked and isn't currently in the way—but maybe Mr Impatience is pre-emptively making sure it won't be in the way when he races off to his next fare. One of the removalist guys comes down the stairs from the house that's the other half of my duplex, and gets in the truck, and it heads off, exactly in accordance with my driver's wish.

I guess that means some new tenants have moved in next door. Again. I wonder how long these ones will last. It's usually students, and they stay for a semester or a year, then move on.

As I'm walking in the door, another ping comes through on the phone. I put down my luggage: Xavier again. *When can we skype?* I wait until I'm lying on the sofa—a sigh escapes me, relief, unable to repress after a fourteen-hour flight—and text back. Definitely too tired tonight. Maybe tomorrow? That's Saturday afternoon here, Friday night there; I recall what he has planned for that evening; there'll rarely be as good an overlap. *Fri night your time, 1am?* I hope I won't be too jetlagged. The return text agreeing to the time comes quickly. I send back a smiley.

AT THE sound of the alarm, I force myself to get up as the Saturday morning sun angles into my bedroom. I want my body clock to readjust as soon as possible, so I've tuned the alarm to a particularly annoying radio station. The two hosts, the inexplicably popular whiny-voiced guy and the faux-outraged woman, are in the middle of one of their typically "controversial" arguments; I jump up and hit the button to send them to oblivion.

So: shower and then stocking up on groceries.

Because I'm relatively early, the supermarket's not too busy, and I get that done fairly quickly. I stop by the bottle shop too and buy a couple of six-packs of beer. One's for the new neighbours, something I've been doing as long as I've been living at my current house. I figure it's nice to be neighbourly, plus they usually reciprocate by letting me know when they'll be having parties and apologizing in advance in case it's inconvenient. And sometimes inviting me, but I've only gone to a couple. Too young a crowd.

The rest of the day is boring chores—sending off a brief yet positive report about the trip, doing all the laundry from my luggage, et cetera—and then it's almost time for my Skype call. I think about what to wear, decide on some going-out clothes; we weren't explicit about it, but I think we're both pretty sure about what will happen. I've never really done the cam thing—cammed—people do use cam as a verb, right?—but it's pretty much the only option that Xavier and I have at the moment, so that's what it will be. So I put on a fairly tight T-shirt and boxer-briefs and jeans, feeling a little weird but basically ready to go.

I look at my watch. Still half an hour until the agreed time. I can drop over the beer. So I take the six-pack, walk down the stairs of my own place in my bare feet and up the stairs of its twin, and knock on the door.

At first I think no one's home. I knock once more and get ready to just leave it there; I can come back and put a note on it saying hi. But the door opens.

A face appears at leg height, which isn't expected. It's covered in some kind of tomato sauce, which also isn't expected. The whole image, sauce and all, looks like it belongs to a five-year-old.

There's an adult too, looking down at the top of the head at his side, saying, "I said, go back to the table, you're still eating."

"You're not at the table, but."

"That's because I have to answer the door, but." He looks up.

It's rare to have that sensation where you think someone is so good-looking that your breath catches. Not audibly, but you can feel your lungs do a little twitch.

He's blond, with hair that looks like it could be curly but that's cropped close, the curls all under control. Blue eyes. His jaw muscles are noticeable, in an attractive way, like he chews gum a lot or grinds his teeth, and it makes for a strong jawline underneath a layer of scruff. He's wearing tradesman clothes, not the high-vis vest, but that kind of dark blue thick denim that's resistant to wear and tear. In his case, it already has a couple of rips on the collar, and his shirt is opened at the top two buttons; there's something stitched on it, some tradesman logo or something, I guess. I'm already looking too long, so I don't try to read it.

"Hi. I'm your neighbour, and I just came over to say welcome—" I hold up the beer. "—but it looks like a bad time."

He looks slightly confused, then holds out his hand. "Paul," he says. He gives me one of those really firm handshakes that seems to be a professional necessity for a tradie.

"Aaron." I wave to the kid. "Hi." He or she doesn't say anything.

Paul looks at the beer. "You don't have to do this."

"It's sort of a tradition now. Usually it's a bunch of students who move in here, and it's good to get off on the right foot."

"Well, this'd be a bit different for you."

"It is a change of pace." I think of that year with Marty—or had his name been Jimmy?—who'd answered the door that first time obviously high, wearing only a T-shirt and a strategically held hat.

The kid starts tugging on Paul's trousers, which are the same dark denim as his shirt. The extra sauce that's now on it isn't too noticeable among the paint splotches. "Dad," the kid says, quietly but emphatically.

"And this is Samantha," he says.

She kicks his leg.

"Sam," he corrects.

"Hi," I say, and hold out my hand to shake. She doesn't take it, but does mumble back a hello.

"Can we go back and have dinner now?" she asks.

Paul looks at me. "Sorry."

"That's fine, really. I didn't mean to interrupt." I hand over the beer and he takes it, I think with a bit of reluctance.

"Okay. You look like you're going out, so I'll let you go." He looks at me. "I'll see ya round, then."

I watch as he distractedly closes the door, and go back home.

It's around 6.15 p.m., which is 1.15 a.m. LA time, and Xavier hasn't answered the couple of times I've tried to call. I figure it's been a bigger Friday night than planned and he isn't home yet; which is fine. It's not a scheduled work meeting.

I reckon the new neighbours are from Queensland. It's not like the US or UK here, where regional accents are super-distinctive. But that sentence-final "but," that's a giveaway. It doesn't narrow it down a lot—they could be from anywhere between urban Brisbane and the Deep North, with all the connotations that that Deep brings with it—but having them as neighbours is indeed likely to be quite different from the usual, which usually runs to hipster twenty-year-olds with the occasional ex-private-school athlete thrown in.

I undo the top button on my jeans. Either Xavier will be coming home, in which case I can get the motor going, so to speak; or he won't, but I'll still feel like getting off. I have the whole Internet at my fingertips if necessary.

It's only five minutes later that Xavier does call. He's pretty drunk, but he smiles charmingly and acknowledges it up front. "Sorry, it was a kind of farewell for Lawrence—remember, he's going back to New York—and we stayed out a bit late."

"No worries," I say, but he's already unbuttoning his shirt, leaving it on but open over his chest. Then, with only a slight stumble and his head going off the screen for a second, he shucks his pants.

He really does have both a good body and a nice face; I lucked out a bit here. His dark hair, normally slicked back, has a few strands falling across his forehead, probably from dancing earlier in the evening if he had anything to do with organizing it. And his chest shows the effects of all the swimming he does; his legs, too, I get reminded as he sprawls in the chair and pushes it away on its casters so I can see all of him, at least from the knees up.

That chair. "Are you in your living room?" I whisper.

"Yes," he faux-whispers.

"Aren't you worried about your flatmate?"

"Flatmate?" He laughs. "No, David's asleep. I can't use the laptop in my room because it's for work, so the only choice is the desktop out here."

I hadn't thought of that. "Do you still want to, mmm, talk, or maybe do it another time?"

"Of course I still want to, mmm, talk." He puts both of his hands down the front of his boxer-briefs—they're white and fit him really well—and the elastic stretches to reveal the hair at the point where it widens out, going downwards from his navel. And then he stretches it some more to give just a glimpse of the base of his cock. "Put your T-shirt up over your head," he says, the earlier casualness having vanished like water on a hotplate. I know what he wants, the way he likes me to have the T-shirt stretched across the back of my shoulders. "And why are your jeans still on?"

I take them off. I'm already pretty much entirely hard inside my briefs, from the earlier stimulation and from being reminded how hot Xavier is. He pulls out his cock first, and I follow.

"I wish you could be putting your mouth around my cock now," he says. I'd rather have the physical contact, too, of course, the touching; but the visuals are enough now, easily enough, and I stop thinking about what I'm missing.

I get startled out of my stroking rhythm when from across the connection there's the sound of a door and a voice asking faintly, "Are you looking at porn?"

Xavier has bent forwards so that the interloper, David almost certainly, can't actually see his hard-on, although the rest of the near-nakedness is a pretty strong clue; but he doesn't seem embarrassed. "No. Just checking some stuff on the Internet."

David says something else and Xavier laughs. Then he turns back to me and laughs again. "He's gone." He sits back in the chair, just as he had been before the interruption, and restarts his strokes.

Unlike him I've gone down to half-hard. "You want to keep going?" I ask.

"Uh, yeah," he says.

So I do. I wonder if David is actually watching, perhaps from behind a door slightly ajar, as I didn't hear it close; I wonder if Xavier is wondering about this. Maybe Xavier likes it. I don't know whether he would.

But I don't think about that; I just look at him, as his neck muscles tighten and he makes that very quiet sound that means two seconds to coming; and I arrive just after he does.

THE NEXT morning starts early, even though it's a Sunday, at my regular cafe. My favourite table at the window is free, the one on the same side as the counter. I sit, and Axel calls out, "You're back! Long black?"

"Yes please. I see spring's arrived while I've been away. Sun and noisy lorikeets, and I can check out your legs in shorts." The place isn't busy yet; the nearest customers are at distant tables.

Axel laughs. I think to myself, not for the first time, that if I heard a guy I didn't know say that to a female waiter, I'm sure I'd immediately frown about potential sexual harassment. But for us it's a long-running joke, and Axel is happy to play along. As he's doing now, stretching upwards theatrically. "Ah, I just need to loosen up after all this intense work." He's only been working fifteen minutes. His T-shirt rides up, just as he intended, to show the planes of his stomach that he keeps flat with constant skateboarding. "If only there were some way I could loosen this tension." I laugh. He's straight.

"So what were you doing again?"

"I was in LA, working with the fire department."

"Oh yeah, that *Minority Report* stuff."

"Sort of." Very sort of. Data analytics, pulling in data from a bunch of places and making it easy to manipulate; nothing at all as fancy as that hologram-grabbing setup in the movie. But close enough for the concept.

"What's the name of your company again? I tried to tell Erica, but forgot again."

Erica's his girlfriend, who I see in here sometimes and have a nodding acquaintance with. I tell him the name again, chosen from *Lord of the Rings* by the founders, Silicon Valley geeks. I'm convinced that part of the reason I got the job was that I knew where it came from. Axel says it to himself, and I'm pretty sure he'll forget it this time too.

I ask him how things have been going while I've been away, and (in a roundabout way) about the mood of the owner today. He's a bit of an explosive individual, the owner; maybe he's watched too much Gordon Ramsay on TV. Today's apparently okay, and Axel can continue along being his usual efficient yet friendly self.

IT'S ALSO a good day to cycle. I don't have too big a breakfast: my appetite doesn't usually come back fully until a couple of days after a long flight in any case, and I've already decided I want to go for a ride.

South, I think. I'll keep to the main roads at the start, across the one minor river first, then onwards to the second one, broader, right where it becomes the bay that meets the ocean. It's only an hour each way, but there's that park where you can sit and watch the water—why does hardly anyone go there?—and that's what I want today.

I go home, get changed, helmet up, collect my bike; then I'm off. It's hard at thirty minutes into the ride, as I expect: LA was an intense two weeks of work, trying to get as much done as possible while I was there, not much time off. And when I did get to the gym, there were the stationary cycle limits of twenty minutes. But a disruption of two weeks isn't so long in the scheme of things, and my body remembers what it's supposed to be doing fairly quickly. I get there in the predicted hour.

I do lie on my back for a while when I first arrive, not paying attention to the water that's part of the point of choosing the place, as I recover my breath from the hills on the way here, but then sit up, drink some more, and look outwards. I love the water.

WHEN I get back, I am, not surprisingly, dripping with sweat. Hunched over the handle bars I roll to a stop outside my house, dismount, and pick up the bicycle to take it up the stairs; look up, and see the new guy standing at my door. Paul.

"Uh, hi." I'm not very articulate after a ride.

"G'day. I just came over to see if you felt like one of those beers you gave me. I mean, I'd normally do turnabout when someone gives me something, but I wasn't expecting that from someone from the city"—my estimate of a Deep North origin increases as he says this—"and wasn't prepared, so I figured the least I could do is share one with you."

"You don't have to, really. But it would be great now. Or at least, after a shower."

"Too easy. Five minutes, then?" Obviously he's an efficient showerer. "Or whenever, really."

I nod, and he makes way for me to go inside. My shower would normally be closer to fifteen minutes after a ride—which I know is pretty decadent, after all those years of being reminded of what a dry continent we live on, but really, it's fairly harmless as vices go—but

I don't want to give the impression of being a wuss. After the shower I put on old loose shorts and an old T-shirt that sags a bit at the neck, as I figure it's likely to be casual over there, and these are my usual comfortable clothes after cycling anyway. Then I head down and up the stairs to their door, and in the end it's probably not too much more than five minutes.

Paul opens the door and flicks his head to indicate I should come in, and I do. It's not the first time I've been inside there—for those student house parties, or helping out the owner between tenants—and in any case it's the mirror image of mine. There's the front room off the hallway, which at the moment seems to be a storage room for boxes, followed by the centre room, which is where the TV is. There are still those gouges in the woodwork from the last batch of tenants, a circular burn mark on the top of the fireplace's wooden frame, and a boarded-up window.

"Hi Sam," I say. *Scooby-Doo* is on. From her beanbag in front of the screen, she doesn't lose her focus on Fred and Daphne's exchange of dialogue for one second. Paul shrugs at me and I smile.

"I'll just be on the back veranda with Aaron from next door, okay?" She still doesn't look. "Okay, Sam?" Louder this time. "Sam." Louder still. She nods.

We go through the kitchen, and he collects two beers from the fridge as we go through, which he hands to me. The kitchen has some scars too, including some exposed wiring. Out the back in the small paved yard there's a full-sized plastic chair, and one mini one; Paul's bringing another chair, also plastic, from the kitchen.

We sit, pop the caps off the beer with the opener Paul has already tied to the back door with string, and take the first sip. Our sighs come almost in unison.

"Long ride?" he asks.

"A couple of hours there and back. Long enough for this to taste pretty good."

"I'd ask where you went, but I still don't really know the city, so it wouldn't mean anything to me." City. He says the word almost capitalized.

"Just south a bit. Sat by the water."

We drink a bit more in silence; I'm happy just to be mellow for a bit while I'm recovering.

"What do you do for a quid, then?"

I don't even crack a smile, manage not to, at the country-boy expression. I mention the company, and try to explain what they do, and what I do. "You know those TV cop shows, where they have some IT person who can hack into anything, find out whatever's needed in the hour-long episode via a couple of keystrokes and some neat graphics on a screen? Abby from *NCIS*, or that occasional guy from *Law & Order*."

"Yeah, nah, I don't know them, but I know the kind of show."

"It's not at all like that in real life, mostly. More like they still use printed-out photos on a pinboard and string linking locations on a map. But we build the sort of stuff that's on the TV shows."

"Cool," he says. Then, "Is the name from *Lord of the Rings*?"

That's unexpected. "Yep. Got it in one."

WE'RE ON our second beer each when Sam comes outside. "I'm hungry," she says.

"How about an apple?"

"Okay. I've still got my wobbly tooth, but."

"How old are you?" I ask.

"Five."

It turns out I'd guessed correctly yesterday. "Wow, that's early to get a wobbly tooth," I say. "Is it your first one?"

She nods.

"Do you have kids?" asks Paul.

"Nope. Just a much younger sister. I was almost twenty when she was this age, and I helped out with her, so I remember it all pretty well."

I try to guess his age. Probably midtwenties. Sam's five. They start early in the country, I guess.

"My mum used to make spaghetti all the time for my sister when her teeth were wobbly because it was easy to eat. And when

10

her tooth came out, she sucked it in through the gap. Does your mum make spaghetti?"

There are storms inland that come on so suddenly, clouds from nowhere and crackling with lightning, dry at first but then releasing a downpour. Sam's face is just like that, just before the waterworks. I've obviously put my foot in it somehow.

"Mum will be coming this afternoon," says Paul quickly. "It'll be soon. How about I put on the *Scooby-Doo* movie for you, and we'll get an apple on the way. Maybe yoghurt."

He steers her with his hand on her back, and he's gone for a while, longer than I think it would take to put on a DVD. I was already close to the end of the second beer, so I finish it off. After a bit more sitting on my part, looking out at the yard that, like the rooms, has a lot of visible marks of former tenants, with a few outdoor toys and a couple of weights for lifting in one corner but not that much else, he returns, apology on his face.

"She wants me to watch it with her. I wouldn't normally, but…. Sorry. I can't ask you to watch *Scooby-Doo*."

Actually, that'd be okay, watching *Scooby-Doo*. But it's seeming like there'll be some calming down that has to take place, and I'll just be in the way.

"That's okay. I do have some stuff to get ready before I go into work tomorrow, so I might as well get on with that. Even though I would rather be in Coolsville with you guys."

He laughs.

Sam is lying on the sofa in the TV room, and Paul's nod is a bit distracted as I head out the door.

CHAPTER 2

EACH RETURN from overseas, I feel like it's a restart of normal life. I haven't switched over to seeing the franticness of the US stints—LA this time, New York the last, others before that—as the way things have to be. Having time for cycling, reading, hanging out with friends, playing bridge when I want some extra burnish for my nerdiness: it doesn't feel right until I have those again.

So it's odd that I'm feeling out of sorts this first week back. It's partly that I'm not catching up with my work friends. Instead, I'm "on the beach" as they say here, using some downtime to pick up new knowledge. In this case it's totally uninteresting new knowledge, which comes to me in the form of a three-day workshop on the implications of the Defence Trade Controls Act.

To be fair to the presenter, she does the best she can with her material. Her surname's Choi—I didn't catch her first name—and she's very composed and good at answering questions, even when they're annoying.

"So how does this make any sense here, this supply-versus-broker thing?" asks the guy next to me. I'd already surveyed the room, and of the dozen here there wasn't anyone I wanted to check out more; but especially this guy, just based on his general sleazeball style. And his personality has only reinforced it. *Yeah, okay, it's boring for all of us*, I think, *but if you'd been paying more attention to the last slide and less to your Facebook feed, you wouldn't have to ask this question and make it longer and more painful for the rest of us.*

That's when I get a text. It's from Xavier, and I smile and open it. It's a dick pic. Christ! I close it quickly. Another part of feeling out of sorts, I think, has been uncertainty with Xavier. I've never had a long-distance relationship before, and it's hard to see where things will go. Still, he is thinking of me. I guess.

I get another text. This one is just words, and we have a short conversation.

X: *send me one*

me: *I'm at a workshop.*

X: *from the bathroom there :)*

me: *No!*

Still, I spend the afternoon in a state of low-level arousal. Unlike my tosser colleague, my lack of attention doesn't make me waste people's time with dismissive questions.

I'm one of the last to leave, and I thank the presenter. There's another two days to go, and I don't want her to feel totally discouraged: she's obviously aware that no one actually wants to be there.

Plus, I have a totally stupid plan that's already making my palms sweaty with nerves. It's an hour until I'm meeting up with Sveta and Howie, my closest friends from uni days, so I don't even have the justification of potentially running late to talk myself out of it.

I go to the bathroom. I'm almost certain everyone's left. When I go in I start with some reconnaissance. You go around a corner, and there's the counter with three basins and a long mirror, and three cubicles directly across from it. Ideal for a stupid, stupid plan. I go into a cubicle, close the door, wait a second, and then open it again: I'm directly facing the mirror, as expected. I go back to the entrance of the bathroom and test the main door, which makes a satisfying squeak that I hadn't been paying sufficient attention to notice before. Then I go back to the same cubicle and close the door.

I'll hear anyone if they come in, I say to myself. I take off my shirt, hang it on the hook on the back of the door, put my T-shirt over my head so it's stretched across the back of my shoulders, and pull down my trousers and boxers to midthigh. I get Xavier's dick pic up on my phone, and it's pretty good for getting things started, but it's not exactly what I want. So I go to a photo of his face, one of him smiling with the more wicked of his two dimples showing, and then use my thumb to flick between them. Flick, stroke, stroke, flick, stroke, stroke. After a while I remember to listen for the squeak of the door, and during the next flicks and strokes I still don't hear anything.

So I change to the camera on my phone and open the door—I'm not sure who would be an appropriate deity to launch a prayer to at this point—maybe Priapus—and after about two seconds of positioning I take the shot and quickly retreat again to the cubicle.

I look at the photo. It's my first mirror selfie of any sort, and I realize there must be some skill to knowing where to look and how to hold the phone. Still, I'm not taking another one, and that's probably not the main thing Xavier will be paying attention to.

I debate whether I should send it. I know the hazards intellectually, although my photographic incompetence means my face isn't very recognizable; I feel both turned on and stupid, the ridiculousness only enhanced by all the tactical scouting and planning necessary for it.

I send it anyway.

HALF AN hour later, in the taxi, I get a photo back, a belly with come sprayed over it, and a "thanks :) ." Quite a lot of come. I guess he liked it.

AS I enter the bar, Sveta is walking towards a bench where Howie's standing, carrying three beers, so I head over in that direction.

Howie gives me a bro hug in welcome; Sveta a hug that fits itself to my body and presses her prominent breasts against me, then a European kiss on each cheek. We clink our bottles together and take a drink. "Cheers."

"So, this guy in LA, Xavier," says Sveta, with only the briefest of pauses to let me settle in. "How are things going? Any photos?"

I go to hand her my phone, and then I think, uh-oh, and take it back. "Just got to go to the bathroom. I'll tell you about him when I get back."

In the bathroom I check that my phone is synched for cloud backup, and after a brief linger on the dick pic and its follow-up, I delete them from my phone. There are still a couple of face pics, and one of the two of us in Santa Monica, taken that middle weekend of the last trip, that I like. I head back to the table.

"Here." I hand over the phone.

"He's cute," she says. "I like the one of you guys on the pier. Lots of energy between you, even with that crowd there."

"Let me look," says Howie. He flicks through them. "Not bad." He does some part-time modelling outside his regular journalist job, is used to objectively assessing other guys' looks, usually from a competitive perspective. He hands me back the phone. "Did you just meet him this trip?"

"It's the same guy from the trip before," interrupts Sveta. In our uni classes together, the guys—and those classes were heavily skewed towards guys—always assumed she must be a bimbo, and didn't realize how sharp her memory and mind were until she shot them down. Now that she's a project manager, I gather the same shooting down still happens.

"Yeah," I say. "He's the one I got to know at the work dinner the last time, and he made me laugh, and we just clicked." And hooked up after the dinner. I remember him sliding his hand into my shirt in the taxi… anyway.

"That sounds like it's going well, then," says Howie. "You know, it's been two months since I've had a girlfriend."

I do know. He mentions it all the time, since until this recent situation, he'd been continuously serially monogamous from the time we all lived together during uni; this current state, he can't believe it.

"I can't believe it." He shakes his head.

"You know, you probably didn't realize it, but before Xavier, I was single for eighteen months. Two months isn't that long."

"I noticed," murmurs Sveta.

"Eighteen months!" Howie says, as unbelieving as if I'd announced the moon was made of cheese. "That's like a total sexual desert. How did you cope?"

His mention of the desert reminds me of this old song, by Everything But The Girl, which draws a parallel between missing someone and the deserts missing the rain. I always thought that was an

15

odd analogy: deserts don't miss the rain. The ecosystem has evolved so it does just fine without rain. For myself, I have my friends, my work, and my books; I don't mind solitude.

That's not to say that there weren't a couple of dips in oases during that eighteen months, but on the whole, the dryness didn't bother me.

"Ech, it wasn't that hard."

"Dude," says Howie, "it must have been hard the whole time." Howie's double entendre is so juvenile that both Sveta and I laugh.

Howie's succession of girlfriends—Katie, Stacey, Jamie before that—were all girls he'd known from uni. They used to hang at our house, just several among a big regular crowd of friends and acquaintances, drink and chat and laugh with us, crush on Howie. I've wondered for a while if Howie himself has noticed the pattern—I'm sure Sveta has—wonder if he's understood what he's looking for. He could easily meet girls in his modelling, does meet them, but this particular well is running dry. Maybe one day the two of us will have to have a drinking session where I do some advice-dispensing.

"Anyway," says Sveta, "how do things feel they're heading with Xavier?"

I have nothing to say on the topic: I have no idea. I shrug. "Maybe I should go to a fortune teller. And speaking of fortune tellers, how's your sister?"

Sveta's older sister Katarina had taken her to a fortune teller as a way of bringing up the issue of children, and specifically the issue of when Sveta was going to have some. Katarina herself has two and runs a day-care centre; children are a central preoccupation of her life. Sveta was so angry she stormed off from the fortune teller's market stall and didn't speak to her sister for a week.

"Ugh," she says. "This week, you'll never guess...."

Conversation successfully diverted.

NOT MUCH happens during the week. The workshops don't become suddenly more interesting. I swap some messages with Xavier—text only this time—which make me laugh. I don't see anything of the new neighbour. It's all dark there by the time I get home: past the bedtime of five-year-olds.

But on Thursday when I get home, there's a note in my letterbox underneath an electricity bill. The handwriting's not what anyone would call neat. COME TO DINNER NEXT DOOR SAT 6PM? TURNABOUT. PAUL.

Sure. When I get inside, I write just that one word on a note, then go back out to stick it in their letterbox.

I SEE Paul on Saturday morning, as I'm heading out for a cycle. "Still okay for dinner?" he asks.

"Indeedy."

"It's not going to be anything fancy."

"Okay, not coming, then. I only come to dinner if there's a guarantee of caviar and champagne."

He laughs. "I've never had either of those."

"Of course not-fancy is fine. You want a hand with anything?"

"Nah, mate."

"See you at six, then."

He nods.

This time I head east, through the downtown area and then out the other side. I avoid Bondi, which will be already heaving with tourists, and go to a beach just south of it. It's early in the season and so not super-packed. I chain up my bike, take off my shoes and socks, and stick them in a plastic bag I brought with me for the purpose, before walking towards the ocean. Dry sand's hot on my feet at first until I get to where the waves, only small ones today, lick up onto the beach. I stand just there, looking out at the horizon for a while.

When it feels like time to go, I walk over to the surf lifesaving clubhouse and rinse my feet under a tap there; it's only about five minutes before the sun's dried them. Then I cycle for another half an hour to a train station and catch the train home.

DINNER IS spaghetti. Paul does seem to have made a bolognese sauce rather than getting one out of a tin. He's holding a beer in a stubby cooler in one hand while he stirs with the other.

"Help yourself." He gestures with his beer hand to the fridge. The beer I gave him is gone, presumably consumed, replaced with a gold-canned Queenslander variety, so I take one of those.

I'd let myself in through the unlocked front door—after calling out a hello and hearing some indistinct reply—and have already seen Sam at the TV. *Scooby-Doo* again.

Paul calls out, "Dinner's ready, so TV off." After a few seconds, Sam comes into the kitchen without complaint. I suspect that might be a Rule.

We all sit at the kitchen table. There are just the three chairs, so I'm guessing the increasingly mysterious Mrs Paul won't be joining us. I don't ask.

"Two four six eight," says Paul.

"Bog in, don't wait," responds Sam.

I raise my beer as contribution to the dinner prayer.

After her first mouthful of spaghetti, Sam says, "I like Velma."

"Me too," I say. "She's my favourite of the gang. It is funny how she always loses her glasses, though. 'Help me, I can't find my glasses!'" I wave my hands around like I'm gesturing blindly. "She should have just glued them to her head."

"You can't glue glasses to your head."

"Yes you can. I just did it today." I'm wearing my glasses this evening rather than my usual contacts.

"No you didn't."

"Yah-huh I did."

She looks at her dad, but he has a neutral face on. Then she goes to get up from her chair, hesitates, looks at Paul again—I'm guessing there might be a Rule about getting up from the table—and then reaches over to my glasses. I put my left hand, the one away from her that she can't see from where she is, on the arm of the glasses, so when she tries to take them off they stay put. She tries again, but I still keep them on. She looks dumbfounded.

Paul laughs.

"Just kidding," I say as I take them off.

"And don't try gluing anything to your ears." Paul tries for a stern look.

"See, I knew you didn't glue them."

"Okay, eat your dinner now," says Paul.

She focuses back on her food. I look at Paul. His jaw muscles look underworked with this dinner, like they should be chewing steak instead. He's wearing the same work shirt with the ripped collar. He does have a solid neck and strong collarbones; his chest, what I can see of it with the two open buttons, looks almost smooth.

Paul asks, "Where did you ride today?"

"The beach," I say.

"There's a beach?" Sam sounds amazed and a bit excited. "And you can go there?"

"Yep. It's a pretty nice one too. I see a lot of kids there."

Sam looks at Paul. "Eat your dinner," he says.

The rest of dinner is pleasant too. After dinner Paul goes to sort out the pre-bed routine for Sam—bath, teeth, et cetera—and I do the dishes after ignoring an attempted demurral by Paul, a half-hearted "Just leave it and I'll do it later."

When he comes back I'm drying the last of the dishes.

"If you like we could watch a DVD. It's not a new one or anything, just one I rented for the weekend. *Troy*."

I've seen it before, ranted about it with Howie and Sveta and Sveta's boyfriend Ted, but it's okay. "Sounds good."

In the TV room, he sits on the sofa; I choose the single armchair. The narrator relates some Trojan War history with a map of Greece as backdrop, and then we see Brad Pitt demonstrating that he is the greatest of the Achaean warriors.

About twenty minutes from the end Paul looks like he's falling asleep but he holds out until the final credits. "Sorry," he says, "late night for a tradie. Not a bad movie, I thought."

"Apart from the terrible things they did to the story. But for what it is, yeah, not a bad movie."

He seems to come awake a bit. "What do you mean?"

I think to myself that this isn't really the time to carry out an extended and likely ranty dissection of the movie. With Howie and Sveta, we had some shared knowledge we could rely on; Paul, though, has told me at dinner about leaving school at fifteen to be an electrician—though he never says electrician, just "sparky," as in, "So yeah, that's how I became a sparky." So any conversation with him would need a different starting point.

"Hey, it's late," I say. "Another time. But this was fun, really. And I enjoyed dinner."

Paul sees me off at the front door, as I go down his stairs and up mine.

THE NEXT afternoon I'm out in the front garden. It's fifteen minutes until a Skype with Xavier, and I'm dressed as I was the last time. I wouldn't normally be doing any garden-related things in these clothes, but I'd just heard a crash, and came out to find that one of the plant pots had been smashed—probably a dog knocking it over, or maybe a very large cat, coming in through the front gate I appear to have left open—and there are sharp fragments all over, and I thought I should pick them up now rather than forget and slice open a sole in the dark later.

That's when Paul comes out his front door. He looks at me. "Are you going out?"

"Uh, no."

"Cool. I can't always tell with what city people wear. Anyway, I was just wondering about the *Troy* story. What was wrong with it?"

Hmm. I only have fifteen minutes. "So the *Iliad* wasn't about the whole Trojan War—"

"The what?"

"The *Iliad*. The story it's based on. It's about Achilles—actually, it's about anger. Briseis is way less important, not the major love

20

interest; she's just a trophy, and it's just Achilles' pride that's dented when she gets taken from him—he's being dissed by Agamemnon. That's what makes it clear that the cost of his anger is so great, because the trigger isn't that important—Patroclus dies because of his tantrum over being dissed. And Patroclus isn't just his cousin." I haven't told Paul I'm gay. I'm out to pretty much everyone, and will be at some stage with Paul, but I figure I should go a bit slower with the country boy. So this isn't the time to get into anything touching on that. "Patroclus is way more important in the story."

I look at my watch. "Sorry, I have to dash. I'm not going out, but I do have a Skype call scheduled for two minutes' time."

"Sorry, mate. I'll let you go, then."

"No worries. I'm always happy to talk about books." I smile.

I go inside and quickly wash my hands, then sit down at the computer. It's then that I see there's a message from Xavier, apologizing, saying he's been caught up and there won't be a call today.

I feel a bit flat. I was looking forward to seeing Xavier, talking. Getting off with him, sure. But not just that.

If I'd seen the message before, I could have kept talking about the *Iliad* instead. It'd seem pretty dumb to go next door now, though. I imagine how I might restart the conversation with Paul. "So to continue this topic that you could well have had no interest in...."

So neither of those. Instead, I bring up the recording I'd made of the last Skype call. That'll have to do.

I take off my jeans, put my shirt over my shoulders, push my briefs down my thighs, and start stroking.

IF I go in to work, it'll still be more workshops. I decide instead to take up one of the other options I have when I'm on the beach, and work from home. I send an e-mail on Sunday night, outlining my plan, and get an OK on Monday morning.

It's always hard when you're explaining potential problems with bringing data together, even—or especially—to the clients who want to do it. I can show an equation on the screen in a presentation, but a tensor product just makes everyone's brains switch off. Demos with coloured graphs and moving parts work much better.

I'm going to make a demo illustrating that problem Netflix had in their challenge. That one where they gave out some data about movie rentals, supposedly anonymized, to see who could do the cleverest stuff with it: the winner would get the prize money, and Netflix would get the clever idea. It was unfortunate for Netflix that the cleverest idea involved some statistical de-anonymization and cross-referencing with IMDb; it managed to uncover the identities of some users, along with the fact that they were fans of *Queer as Folk* or Noam Chomsky documentaries. Netflix pulled the data and the prize.

It's fun to do, writing some code and making the demo; it's also fun that I can do it at my own pace. After I've made some progress, I can go for a walk in the park and get a coffee, and have a new idea about how I should present the demo.

I also start to learn Paul and Sam's routine. They get home around 4.30 p.m., from day care, I assume. Still no sign of Mrs Paul: so maybe there's no Mrs Paul on the scene after all. No point being nosy; I suppose I'll hear eventually. I put up my hand so they can see it through the front window where my desk is, wave hi as they go inside.

On Wednesday I'm out the front weeding. I like weeding—it feels satisfying, and only engages a part of my mind, the rest of which can be free. Like cycling, I guess. Paul and Sam come home at the usual time; I say hi, and they both say hi back before going inside.

Paul comes out again after about five minutes.

"You know, I don't know how anyone can read this *Iliad*. It's really repetitive. 'He fell, thunderously, and his armour clattered upon him.' How often do they say that?"

He's still in his work clothes, the same ripped shirt, unless they're all ripped in the same place. I sit back on my feet, knees splayed outwards.

"People who know about that stuff say they're just the signs of how it used to be an oral epic." I hesitate. "Do you really want me to tell you this?" He nods, so I continue. "Anyway, the storyteller would have some standard phrases—because you had to remember the whole thing—and he could string them together to fit the rhythm he needed when he was reciting it. There was this guy, an anthropologist, about a hundred years ago, who studied storytellers in Eastern Europe who did that exact thing, and he argued that the *Iliad* was retold the same way. So if you think about it as a memory and rhythm thing, it helps. Well, it helped for me anyway."

"How do you know this stuff?"

"I just had someone tell me about it. In my case, a teacher. So I'm just passing the same things along to you."

He nods, thoughtful, seeming to accept that. "My teachers were crap. I'm pretty sure none of them would have known about this."

I try to imagine what a northern Queensland school in the middle of all the cattle stations there would have been like. I can't, really.

I DECIDE I'll go to bridge this evening if it's on. It's pretty casual, and whether it is on or not depends on everyone's availability, which suits me since I'm out of the country too often to be a reliable player. It'll be at Lance's, almost certainly: he's been hosting these since before I met him at a tournament in my late teens. I call, and Lance tells me it is on at his house. It's only five of them, now plus me, and I'm the last to let him know, so I probably won't get a heap of playing time, but that's okay.

It's a moderate walk to their place, but it's good exercise, and also means I can take a bottle of wine and have a wild and crazy night. When I knock, Lance answers. As I expected he's cooking; "just something small" he always says, but it's always good. I present him with the wine—I brought something nice, a cabernet sauvignon, because I appreciate the food—and kiss him hello on the cheek. He smiles back.

I do like him. He's an editor; sometimes we'll just hang around and talk about books, or people, or life. His partner, Doug, is a doctor, and nice enough too, but Lance and I get on especially well.

I go into the front room where the playing table is. The cards have just been dealt, so they're not in the middle of a game, although it's almost certainly not the first game of the evening.

Doug: "Hi."

Fred: "Hello there."

Oliver: "Sweetie!"

James starts singing Adele's "Hello."

I'm the youngest in this group, and among all the bridge players who come along, by about twenty years.

James says, "We haven't seen you in forever!" He often speaks in exclamation points.

"No, I've been in LA for work. Anyway, I'll let you play, and I'll go and help Lance with the food."

"We can swap at the end of the rubber," says James. "I don't want to give up my rubber, I might need it!" I smile as if it's not the hundredth time I've heard that joke.

I go into the kitchen and convince Lance he should let me help him put some salad in a bowl, but first we crack open the wine and pour five glasses—Fred doesn't drink—and we carry in the glasses and some bread and baba ghanoush.

"I knew *you'd* have the queen," James is saying to Oliver. Oliver looks up as we come in and rolls his eyes. He's heard this joke a hundred times too. Still, the predictability is nice in a way: the sun comes up each morning, and James makes the same jokes every bridge game.

"So did you meet anyone in LA?" Lance is asking.

"Actually, I did."

"Do you have any photos?"

"Actually, I do."

"Well, come on, show them around!" says James. He's put his hand facedown on the table.

"Can we finish this hand?" asks Fred.

James sighs exaggeratedly.

"Food's almost ready, I think." Lance nods. "I'll go help bring out things, and tell you about him over dinner."

I go back and help with the salad while Lance asks about things that won't spoil the great relationship revelation over dinner. I tell him about the work in LA, and my Defence Trade Controls Act workshops here, and my new neighbour who's an electrician but who is interested in the *Iliad*. I don't mention anything about Paul's looks.

We take the food in, and everyone clears some space—the hand is finished—so we can eat.

"Give!" says James. So I pass around my phone with the photos of Xavier, the ones left after the editing for Sveta's viewing.

"Oh my God, he's gorgeous," says Oliver.

"You slut!" says James to me. Really, that's not something I'd say to someone I know as casually as James, but to each his own.

The conversation turns to long-distance relationships and how they've worked, or not worked, for each of them. Doug and Lance haven't had any—they've been together for twenty-five years, and I gather it was the first serious relationship for each of them. Fred surprises me by talking about one he'd had which had lasted four years, just by letter writing and phone calls in the days before Skype.

After dinner I'm feeling mellow. We rearrange ourselves and I'm partnering Oliver. We don't play anything fancy, mostly just Standard American bidding, so it's all easy. I look at my hand. "One spade."

XAVIER AND I have another Skype call lined up for Saturday at 4.00 p.m. He doesn't call, doesn't answer. Then, or at 5.00 p.m., or 6.00 p.m., although I'm just waiting that last time, not calling; that already seems desperate enough.

At just before midnight, I get a text. I skim it: a Dear-Aaron message. "It's not you, it's me," blah blah; the tyranny of distance— well-known phrasing that reminds me he's read a bit about Australia— blah blah. It's just before 5.00 a.m. there: I imagine him writing it, slightly remorseful, perhaps slightly guilty and making his way home from someone's house, doing the walk of shame. I don't know, but that's one scenario.

It really was impractical, this long-distance arrangement. And it's not as if I knew Xavier that well—it was more just taking a punt, hoping it might work out rather than expecting it to. It's a good thing I don't get my expectations up too high.

So my rational mind goes.

I find Everything But The Girl and put it on. The song's actually called "Missing." It isn't really right, this song about absences evoking deserts—it's about some longer, more serious relationship, one which prompts walks past the lover's old house, years later—but the melancholy sound is. I think about the desert.

The deserts that don't need the rain.

I'm the fennec fox, with the large heat-dissipating ears.

I'm the kangaroo rat, coming out at night.

I'm the camel, surviving for weeks without a drink.

I'm made for the desert.

CHAPTER 3

THE NEXT morning, I go later than usual for breakfast to the cafe. It's busy, as I planned, and Axel is too busy to talk, also as I planned. I don't want to banter. But he does give me a friendly smile, which is nice, and then brings over my coffee, without asking. It's already a hot day, unseasonably hot. A great day for going to the beach, or the park, or any of those things I don't feel like doing. I head home after breakfast.

I've only been there for a while, pottering around without achieving anything, when there's a knock at the door. It's Paul.

"Uh, can I ask a favour? I just stuffed up some repairs, and I've gaffed it up so it'll hold for a bit, but it's kind of dangerous. And I can't take Sam to the suppliers with me because it's dangerous there too, lots of sharp metal, and I can't leave her in the car on a day like today."

I just look at him. He runs his hand through his short hair, ending up with his palm at the back of his neck, his elbow up in the air at an argh-I-don't-know-what-to-do angle. He looks like he might have cut himself on that wrist.

"It'd only be half an hour. I can be in and out."

"I'm gay," I say.

He pauses. "Does that mean no?"

"No." I think of how this explanation might go—I think you're a yokel, and there's a chance you might freak out if you had discovered this after the fact of me minding Sam, and that even if your fears are unfounded and uninformed, they could completely shape our interactions after this, and you've only just moved in, and that's why I'm blurting this out now, all rushed and unprepared, just in case—but I haven't worked out a polite way of putting this, and he is in a hurry. "I mean, sure, I'll mind her."

"There's nothing to do, really. She's just watching more *Scooby-Doo*. Just keep her out of the kitchen, mainly. And I'll be back soon."

"Okay." As we go down the steps, I ask, "Do you want a Band-Aid or something for that hand?"

He looks at it, surprised. "Nah." Maybe he hadn't noticed.

When Paul's driven off in his ute, I go inside, and Sam is in front of the TV, as expected. It's just at the end of an episode—the janitor has been unmasked, again—and that appears to be the end of *Scooby-Doo*: the theme music for *Dora the Explorer* comes on.

She turns around and sees me. "Hello," she says. "Dora's stupid."

"I think Dora's okay. You can learn some Spanish. *Gracias. Arriba.*"

This doesn't appear to win her over to the show. "There are all these stupid bits where she's not saying anything, like we're supposed to say something instead. Of course she can't hear us."

"That's true," I say. "Do you know where the DVDs are with the movies? We could watch those."

"I don't know where they are," she says. "I'm five."

Hmm. It's only been two minutes and I'm failing already. I can't go ferreting around for movies or books in this house that isn't mine. I could tell her to go and play with some toys, but I don't know how that would go. I take the remote control and flick through channels— not many of them, they don't have cable—and hit on a rerun of *Xena: Warrior Princess*.

"Do you know Xena?" I ask.

Sam shakes her head.

"She's a warrior princess," I say.

"A princess?" She makes a disgusted face.

"A warrior princess. She's an awesome warrior." Just at that moment she's uttering her war cry and delivering a kick to a brigand chief. "That's her."

"Really?" Sam looks intrigued.

"Yep. And that's Gabrielle, her sidekick."

28

Silence descends on the room, apart from the sounds of boots making contact with hokey leather costume armour.

PAUL'S RETURN is about forty minutes later. He comes in, looks at the TV, and smiles.

"I'll explain in a minute," I say. "We're just watching the end of this episode."

He nods and heads out to the kitchen, and shortly there's some banging from that direction. Sam turns up the TV volume.

At the end of the episode I look up, and Paul's standing in the doorway. "Time for afternoon tea," he says. Sam dutifully turns off the TV, and we head into the kitchen.

"Beer?"

"Sure," I say. A beer's just right with the weather as it is. I look around; I think there's been a change to where there'd been some exposed wiring before. It looks like Paul's solved whatever was stressing him, so he probably feels like a beer too.

We head out to the chairs in the backyard, Sam included. She sits for a while, eating her banana, and then jumps up to go and kick a ball. She tries out a war cry, and I laugh.

"We ran out of *Scooby-Doo*," I say, "and that's all I could come up with as an alternative. Sorry."

He laughs too. "No worries." He watches Sam for a bit, then looks up at the sky. "My wife—" he starts. "Sam's mum—" Sam doesn't seem to be listening. "We've split up—that's why you haven't met her—and most of the time it's okay, but sometimes I get stuck. I'm used to having someone else around, so I can do things like duck out to the hardware and get what I need, but when it's just me, it's all those little things that don't work anymore. So I'm really sorry I just dumped this on you." He turns his clear blue gaze on me, looks me in the eyes. "Thanks, mate. I appreciate it."

"No worries," I say in turn, and clink bottles with him.

There's no mention of the gay thing.

Sam tries out her war cry again: it's getting better.

IT'S A couple of days later when he invites me over for dinner again, to say thanks. I tell him he doesn't have to, but I am glad to keep occupied. Dinner is spaghetti again, but this time the sauce is cream with some bacon in it and a few other things, some even green. An approximate *boscaiola*.

Sam isn't watching TV this time when I come in. That's probably not a bad thing—not that I want to be judgmental. It must be hard for Paul, trying to juggle everything. And it's unlikely he was immersed in the whole idea of ultimate parental virtue being attained via infant enrichment activities: that was probably more my own upbringing, even more so for my sister Cordelia. I remember her being shielded from any TV until primary school except for DVDs with visualizations of Mozart sonatas; remember having to read to her all the time. Fortunately I didn't mind reading.

Paul's in the kitchen again and gestures as before to the fridge. Sam comes in from the backyard, looking hot and cross. "Is dinner ready yet?" she asks.

"Not too long," says Paul.

"Can I watch TV?"

"No, dinner will be ready soon."

"But it's not ready now."

Paul seems to have made his decision, and to not want to change his mind. Looking at Sam's face, which he can't see, I'm betting there'll be an explosion soon.

"Do you have any books?" I say to her.

"A couple," says Paul. "There's *The Cat in the Hat*."

She frowns. I start reciting, getting into the Dr Seuss rhythm right from the first words.

"Hey, you know it," she says. It's funny how it sticks even after ten years.

"I do, because I like it and I read it lots with my little sister. Should we read it?"

"Okay," she says.

"Do you know where it is?"

"Yes." She trots off to get it.

"Hopefully that will keep her happy until dinner," I say to Paul.

"It seems to be working so far."

She comes back with the book and hops up into her chair at the table. I sit where I sat last time and start reading.

Dinner is ready a bit before the end, and Paul has plated it up but waits until we've finished the book before putting it on the table. And then we tuck in. I start on the beer that I've left sitting until now.

There's the usual bedtime routine—this time I don't bother asking about the dishes and just do them—which all goes quietly. When Paul comes back, he gets two more beers out of the fridge and gestures into the TV room, although I don't think there'll be a movie tonight: it's a work night. We take the same seats, him on the sofa and me on the chair. He puts on some music, total country. I smile to myself.

After a while he says, "Kaylee, that's my wife, she takes Sam for a week, and then I have her for a week. That's the plan, anyway. Kaylee's still settling in, so Sam's been here more often, although we are swapping her over this Friday for the weekend. We'll have to work out something more permanent later, especially when Sam goes to school."

"That sounds kind of complicated. For you, I mean." Obviously I don't want to make any sweeping pronouncements without having any real idea of the situation. Maybe Paul is actually a jerk and the breakup is mostly his fault, although I haven't seen signs yet of jerkiness. At this stage I just want to show some fellow-feeling. "You seem like you're coping."

"I guess." He takes a drink. "Anyway, I thought I'd just let you know, since it's already meant I've had to ask you for help. Which reminds me to say thanks again."

"Really, it wasn't a problem. Sam is cool."

"She's still trying out that battle yodel. Apparently she took some kids at day care by surprise with it."

I laugh.

"Kaylee's brother is gay," he says, after a period of silence. I raise my eyebrows, inviting further explanation for this random comment. "You know, so it's not that I don't know anyone who's gay. Even though it was pretty unusual where I grew up. I don't mean—yeah, just not the usual thing." The next drink is a long one; his Adam's apple rises and falls, rises and falls. "You're really not much like him, but. Except for clothes you wear sometimes."

I could say that assuming we would be alike is like assuming all Chinese people are alike, or all Muslims; his statement is the kind of thing that everyone I know would consider to verge on gauche. But that sort of conversational smacking down isn't really my style, and I'm happy for him to gradually come to his own conclusions.

"He hit on me, once. After I was already going out with Kaylee."

"Did you deck him?" I think I manage to sound neutral, but I hope he didn't do it.

"No," he says, scornfully, looking at me. "But I really couldn't be around him after that."

Well, that sounded like a warning to me: noted and filed. I don't get my back up.

A new song starts. "Who's the music?" I ask, to change the topic.

He looks incredulous. "Lee Kernaghan?" The intonation implies that I must have just had some temporary memory lapse.

I do know that he's an Australian country singer, but really, I couldn't tell you anything about him. "I'm afraid I'm pretty clueless about his music. What songs of his should I know?"

The conversation takes an easier turn.

THE NEXT day I'm back in the office, about to have a break for morning tea. I have my mug and my teabag, and am just about to go for hot water when I get a call from Sveta.

"Have you heard from Howie this morning?"

"Nope, nothing."

"He can't come to Boney M. on Saturday. He called me to see if there's anyone I can sell his ticket to, but I couldn't think of anyone."

She has a pretty extensive network, so he'd usually try her first for something like this. "I said I'd call you."

"Why can't he go?"

"Some modelling thing that came up. He says. Maybe he just double-booked and forgot."

"Can't think of anyone."

"That's okay. It's his problem. Anyway, how are things with Xavier?"

Christ, she's a busybody. "Kaput."

"What?"

"Kaput. Finished. *Okonchennyy*."

"Thank you for the helpful Russian translation, it was even almost correct. Anyway, sorry about Xavier."

"Me too. Not that much, though. Didn't get too invested."

"Well, we'll just make sure Saturday is fun."

"Sure. Gotta go now. *Do svidanya*." My rudimentary Russian phrases I've learned from a combination of Sveta, Russian literature classes, and Colossus from *X-Men* comics. Sveta finds them entertaining.

"*Do svidanya*."

I go into the kitchen to get some hot water for my tea. Dean is there, probably my closest colleague, at least in terms of what we work on. He's the guy that the company trots out when it wants to emphasize academic credentials. Not because he's the only one with the right skills—a few of us have pretty similar backgrounds—but because he completely looks the part of an absent-minded professor. He'll typically have forgotten to comb his prematurely white hair or tie his mismatched shoelaces or fold down his collar. He is a good guy, though.

"Aaron." He nods.

"Hey." I fill my mug.

"You were just in LA, right? Did you meet Xavier?"

The expression on his face makes it apparent he wants to be helpful, but Christ, not more busybodying, please. "I know the name. I'll have to look him up. Did I mention that for the next time I go back

I'll do a demo on privacy? I was thinking of using Laplacian noise in the statistical model. What do you reckon?"

Dean has strong opinions on Laplacian noise.

Later, as I walk back to my desk, I have an idea. I text Sveta. *Hold Howie's ticket. Will call you this evening.*

I GET home about eight. Paul's probably still awake. I knock on the door, and he answers it in a T-shirt and loose pants that may or may not be specifically designed as pyjamas.

"Hi," I say. "I don't want to keep you up or anything, but do you know who Boney M. is? The band?"

"Yeah," he says in an as-if-I-wouldn't tone. "My parents listened to them a lot. 'Daddy Cool.' 'Ma Baker.'"

"They're actually going to be playing just around here on Saturday night, and one of my friends already has a ticket and can't go. I think you said you wouldn't have Sam, so do you want to go?"

He looks a bit doubtful. "I dunno."

Maybe he's not flush with cash, having just moved. "The ticket's already paid for," I say, "and it'll just be wasted." I'll pay Howie.

"You sure?"

"I'm sure. I'll tell him you can take the ticket?"

"Okay, then."

"Okay. G'night."

"Night."

I call Sveta when I get in. "I've sorted out the ticket. I have a new neighbour, just settling in—he's a bit of a country boy. Boney M. seemed like something he might like. And yeah, he said he'll come."

"Okay. What's he like?"

"Just, country. Has a kid. Didn't deck his brother-in-law for making a pass at him." As I make this last comment, I really don't know why I'm saying it. It starts as a joke, but without context it just makes him sound like a jerk. "No, he's a nice guy."

"Okay." This time the word is infused with dubiousness.

34

"Okay. Just meet outside the theatre as we'd originally planned?"
"Okay."

ON SATURDAY afternoon I'm upstairs and I hear banging from Paul's next door. It could be more fixing up inside, but it sounds louder. I look out the window halfway up my staircase, which overlooks their otherwise private backyard. From there I've previously seen the marijuana seedlings grown by Marty (or was it Jimmy?), the tie-dyeing of shirts by the tenants before that, the tents put up for extra sleeping space by the tenants before that. Now it's Paul who's hitting some large metal kettledrum thing with a large mallet. He's singing something at the same time; it sounds familiar, from after dinner the other night. Lee Kernaghan, singing about piling into the ute on a Saturday night. Paul has a decent voice.

I watch him for a while, but still don't end up having any idea of what he's doing.

I read a bit, then go and have a shower and get dressed, then go and knock on his door. When he opens the door—well, it's funny. In one way he's dressed down. It's all blue, darker for the jeans and lighter for the shirt, as if he doesn't want to draw too much attention, blue everywhere: that's country. In another way, though—the shirt is slim fit, and it fits him really well. The wide cuffs are flicked back, and emphasize his forearm muscles. The jeans—I hadn't realized how long his legs are. He's shaved off the usual scruff and looks—that's enough, I say to myself. Just stop.

"Ready?" I ask.

"Yep."

As we walk down the street, I ask, "What were you working on today? I heard all the noise." He obviously just had a shower—he's all fresh smelling. If he's wearing cologne it's subtle, and I don't recognize it. Maybe it's just him.

"A barbecue. I could buy one, but I like the ones you can light a fire inside and sit by in winter. I was getting the shape right today; next I'll solder a plate on for the top. It's something I can work on while Sam's not here. Old mate down the road gave me the drum cheap." I translate "old mate" to "this guy."

"Did that go okay, the handover yesterday?"

"Yeah, it was okay."

Switch. "So it's an early concert, and we can grab something to eat after that. My friend Sveta's probably made a plan."

"Sure."

When we arrive, Sveta's already there, with her boyfriend Ted, an engineer. I know him reasonably well, and we hang out, although not as often as I do with Sveta. She hands us our tickets and looks at Paul appraisingly. "Sveta, Paul." They shake hands; she and I hug as usual. We go inside.

THE CONCERT'S a lot of fun; Paul's appreciation seems totally genuine, not tinged with the sense of ironic enjoyment that prompted the rest of us to get the tickets in the first place. The first few songs get everyone warmed up. Then, along with the rest of the crowd when the song comes on, we chant "Ra-ra-rasputin," Sveta in an exaggerated Russian accent. I think if Paul had been wearing a cowboy hat, he would have flung it in the air at that point.

AFTER THE concert we gather on the footpath outside.

"I've arranged to meet Howie at the Imperial," says Sveta.

I frown at her. "The Imperial?" It's a bit full-on for Paul, I think, the rainbowiest place in the area. "It's a bit of a walk." Fifteen minutes at most; but what I want is just to go somewhere quieter with fewer drag queens for what I think is his first evening out locally.

"Well, I've already made the plan with Howie." She turns to Paul. "You know, it's where they filmed part of *Priscilla, Queen of the Desert.*"

Ah. So it's not just a coincidence, it's her naturally up-front style. Why let someone dip their toe in the water when you could push them in instead?

Paul just nods. "Uh-huh."

So we walk there, and the Imperial's its normal self. Drag shows don't start until later, so it's just an early evening crowd hanging out and drinking to a backdrop of rainbow flags and glitter. We spot a standing table with a view of the door, so we can see Howie arriving, and grab it before another couple of guys who looked about to take it.

I go to buy drinks. It'll be cider for Sveta and a craft beer for Ted; there certainly won't be any of Paul's Queensland beer here, so I make a guess about what's closest. I look back at them all. Sveta's in the middle, Paul leaning against the wall on one side of her and Ted resting his arms on the table on the other. Their relationship would look ambiguous to an outsider—Sveta could be with either of the guys—so probably Paul won't get hit on.

As I'm in the bar queue considering this, I feel a hand on my shoulder blade, which runs down to the small of my back.

"Sorry, just squeezing through." He's a handsy one: there's a pretty big gap behind me. Still, you've got to admire directness. I smile at him—he's definitely worth a look, straight dark hair with brown eyes and a fit body.

"No worries."

"You here by yourself?"

"No, with friends." I nod over towards them. "I'm buying this round."

"Well, if you feel like joining us later…." With his head he indicates a group of five guys across the room.

"Maybe." I smile again so my non-committal response doesn't seem unfriendly. Then it's my turn to order.

When I bring the drinks back to the table, Paul asks, "So is old mate a friend of yours?"

"Uh, yeah."

"No," says Sveta, "it's just someone who thinks Aaron is hot."

I frown at her, again. Really, there's pushing someone in the water, and then there's holding their head under.

That's the point at which Howie arrives, which is probably a good thing; he comes over towards me. His hair is slicked back:

37

maybe it was a shoot where he was supposed to look like an East Asian Valentino. It's funny when he and Paul see each other—there's a brief but immediate pause for evaluation. In Howie's case it's the assessment of Paul's looks. I don't know if he thinks of it this way to himself, but that's my interpretation: am I better looking? I think it's a dead heat, myself. Then it conjures up for me recollections of *Zoolander*, the face-off between Derek and Hansel over who's the best model, the best looking. I laugh. Howie looks at me and bends his head towards me, and I murmur to him, "Do Blue Steel." He laughs too—he's fine with being ribbed about it. In the movie when they have their confrontation it comes down to a contest where the winning move involves whipping out underwear without removing trousers first. I don't suggest this.

I don't know what Paul's thinking.

Howie reaches over to shake Paul's hand and it's obvious he gets the tradie grip in response.

Funnily, in five minutes' time, they're getting along like a house on fire. I probably should have guessed. Howie's a country boy as well, although from out west, and even though his growing up would have been pretty different from Paul's—his parents owned the town's Chinese-Australian restaurant rather than a cattle station—there seems to be a lot of shared experience, utes and footie and horses. Over the years, the signs of Howie's rural upbringing, the sounds of his origins, have faded, been submerged into the current citizen of Metrosexual Central. So it's funny to hear those telltale signs come back so strongly; I'm reminded of when we first met. I smile.

Sveta seems more relaxed too. Maybe she's decided she's done enough of the confrontational, you-have-to-instantly-adjust approach; maybe she's just letting Howie be good cop. It's nice that she's thinking of me, but I prefer the way things are going now.

I ask Ted about the latest bridge he's building.

CHAPTER 4

THE NEXT day I'm on my front porch, sitting on the bench I have there, half reading and half watching the world go by. It's the monthly market day at the local park, so there's a parade of people walking along the usually quiet street. Purple mohawks, baby-doll dresses with full-sleeve tattoos, Bettie Page lips on whitened faces. Sometimes all on the same person.

Paul sticks his head out his front door. "G'day," he says to me while eyeing one of the passers-by.

"Hey."

"Do you reckon you could give me a hand for a couple of minutes? It's just with a gutter."

I'm wearing old clothes suitable for gutter handling. "Sure."

I follow him through his house. He's wearing a faded grey electrical supplies T-shirt, maroon footie shorts, and Blundstone boots whose elasticated sides are so stretched they seem to have little role in keeping the boots on his feet. A funny thing about footie shorts out in the country is the way they seem impervious to fashion. If you look at urban photos, you see the super-tight and super-short shorts for men from the 1970s; they somehow evolved to the long shorts of recent times where it wasn't the done thing to show your knees, unless you were gay of course; now showing knees is okay, but not much more. The original footie shorts aren't as short as a typical Mardi Gras parade outfit, but they show a lot more skin than regular shorts now. So I see that Paul definitely doesn't have the chicken legs look that about half the guys at my gym have. His legs are long and lean but solid at the same time. His quads contract and release as he clomps through to the backyard.

Out there there's a regular ladder and a stepladder. "So all I need," he says, "is for you to hold this gutter while I drill some holes." There's a new piece of guttering sitting vertically against the fence.

"Okay." I climb onto the step ladder and he hands it up to me. I hold it roughly where it seems it should go—the old guttering's already been removed, leaving a gap—and he climbs the other ladder and adjusts it. When he's happy with it, he picks up his cordless drill from the roof and drills a series of holes.

"Just screws now," he says.

That's less noisy than before, so I say, as he's screwing the gutter on, "You're doing a lot of work for a tenant." Maybe he's getting some discount on the rent for it.

"Actually, I'm not a tenant. Not exactly. The owner wanted to do it up after it'd been run down with all the students, so we've set up this arrangement where I'll get a share of the equity if I do a good job fixing it up. I met him on another job where he hired me, and we just got talking about this."

Not another vanishing renter, then. "Cool."

He brings back a couple of beers from the kitchen, and we sit. This time it's beer in bottles. Still Queensland, though.

"Thanks for the night out. Boney M. were huge. Your friends were good too."

"Yeah, sorry about the Imperial. It can be a bit over the top." I'm picking at the label on my bottle.

"No worries." He pauses. "That Howie. Are you, y'know?"

I look up from my bottle. "What?"

"Close."

"We've known each other pretty much since he moved here. And we lived together for a few years. So yeah, close."

"Yeah, nah, y'know, eh?"

It probably should have clicked before, but it only does just now. I laugh. "Okay, I know what you mean now. No, never. You met him during a brief window of time where he doesn't have a girlfriend."

"Right."

THE COMPANY'S decided to try out pair programming. So instead of working away by ourselves writing code, we do it in pairs. It's mostly for the software engineers, whose job pretty much consists of that. Dean and I only write code as a small part of what we do; for us it's more designing algorithms and working out how the analytics should work. But we decide to try it out too. Apparently the approach to be taken is to introduce it by encouragement rather than by fiat, more carrot than stick. So we all get a "Hey, this will be totally cool" e-mail, and Dean and I decide it'd be good to be supportive.

Sometime before Monday morning, everything's been rearranged to support it. Desks have been joined together, and we have two computers and two monitors and two chairs at each one. The computers have been linked up, so we're sharing a common workspace. We each have a mouse and mouse pointer, but we can move it across to the window that the other one's working on, see what they're doing. Dean and I spend the first few minutes just doing that, opening applications on each other's screen. Kind of juvenile. Then the pair programming evangelist comes out and gives us a mercifully short speech about how it will work and how brilliant it will be. Our productivity will double, our at-work happiness will triple. We're going to start by identifying what we should work on, on this, our first day of the pair programming that will change our lives.

Dean and I have already decided to work on the statistical models in the privacy demo I'd been working on by myself. We've talked about it before, so it seems like an easy place to start. We work side by side for the first hour, and then discuss how our modules will interface. It turns out they won't. There'd been a misunderstanding about one of the function parameters.

At this point of my normal solo programming, I'd go and surf the web, read a blog for fifteen minutes before coming back to the problem. That's not something you can do when you're working in a pair. I have a sudden image of Mormon missionaries: they're sent out in pairs precisely so they can't get up to the sort of mischief they might fall into if they were solo. For them it's sex or jerking off. Here it's just reading about the latest book releases. But that won't wash, so we get straight back into sorting out the problem.

By the time lunch comes around, I'm exhausted. At the tables in the cafeteria with people who haven't taken part in the pair programming trial, there's the usual level of animated conversation, about a show on Netflix or some new ultrathin screen for some device. At our tables, the tables where we guinea pigs are slumped and eating listlessly, there's little conversation at all.

The afternoon's worse. Dean and I snap at each other near the end of the day.

I've only signed up for a week of this, I say to myself as I head home.

The next day is worse. We make sure to be very clear in our discussions about the interfaces in our code, but by the afternoon, the discussion is through gritted teeth. *Why can't he just see what's in my head and realize that's the best way*, I laugh tiredly to myself as I'm on the train home. By the time I arrive at my house, I've decided something will need to be different for tomorrow. A longer lunch break, and before eating I'll go for a short swim at the pool up the road from the office. I call Dean, and he thinks it's a good idea, although he won't be swimming.

So the next day, I have something to look forward to in the middle of the day, and we're also getting more used to talking as we go. So instead of two hours solo with a catch-up at the end to discover the problems, we discuss as we realize that there are alternatives and a commitment needs to be made to one. Not every five minutes—you still need solid time to get anything done—but more often. Then the swim works just as I'd hoped: the rhythm of it relaxes me, and I'm almost as fresh as the morning when the afternoon session starts.

Thursday goes by quickly. At the end of it we have a nice piece of code, and the evangelist is very excited. Admittedly, he's very excited about many things, but we're willing to be congratulated. So it turns out I can adjust my style from the solo work I've become accustomed to. It makes me reflect on other aspects of my life.

I also find out that I'll be going to LA again shortly, to work some more on the LAFD project on the ground. I'll be able to fold in some of what we've just done. Cool.

I STOP by Paul's that evening. "I'm off to LA Friday for two weeks. I thought maybe this Saturday I could show you a few things in the neighbourhood so you get to know it a bit. Maybe breakfast at a local cafe that has a good space for kids—Sam'll be with you, right?—and then just hang out at the park, check out the playground and play some footie with my friends."

"Yeah. Sam will be here, and I think she'll like that. Is it Howie and Sveta and Ted, or different friends?"

"Them plus probably a couple of others."

SATURDAY MORNING we head to the cafe at eight. It's early for the cafe, before there'll be a crowd; I wonder briefly if it's too early for Paul and Sam and if they'd prefer to sleep in, but then I think, a five-year-old and a tradie, they probably think of this as the middle of the day.

Axel kisses me hello and shows us to a table near the kid play area, bringing some glasses of water. After he's gone Paul asks, "So are you and he, y'know?" A small smile tells me the wording is deliberate.

"Nope. He has a girlfriend."

"Jeez. I thought the most confusing thing about the city would be your rabbit-warren streets."

I laugh.

"Hey, Sam," I say, pointing, "this here is all just for kids. There's some animals, and blocks to make stuff with." She looks over to assess it, and seems satisfied. As she gets up I say to her, looking at Paul, "Do you know what you want for breakfast? Eggs? Bacon? Pancakes?"

"I like eggs." She sits down next to the bucket of large Lego-like bricks. "Can I watch *Xena* with you later?"

"Sure. You can watch it with your dad too, though."

"He doesn't know anyone. He doesn't even know Joxer."

I shake my head at him, *tsk*ing. "You don't even know Joxer."

"Okay, I'm hopeless."

Axel comes back and we order.

"On the topic of, y'know—" He smiles again. "—I wondered about Achilles and Patroclus. The book doesn't say, but when Patroclus's ghost comes back, and wants their ashes buried together—that's intense."

"Yeah, it is intense." He must have read just about all of it; that's near the end. I remember that part well, the plea for the ashes together in that golden urn, and the impression it made on me when I first read it. "It's ambiguous, on purpose, I think. But there were lots of ancient Greeks who thought they were, y'know. There was this one playwright who described them as having a devout union of the thighs." Aeschines.

"Also something that didn't get mentioned at my school."

"Yeah. There's this line from a movie that I thought was funny. There are some students doing translation from ancient Greek to English, and the teacher says something about leaving out the part about the unspeakable vice of the Greeks. It was there, but deliberately hidden." I have a drink of water. "A lot of my friends from school had their first inkling of what they liked from their dad's old *Penthouse* or the Internet. This is what it was for me." I laugh. "That's pretty dorky, I know. But there was this guy I had a crush on too, which is probably more normal." That's about enough of mentioning my first boyfriend, Trent.

"Look at what I've made, Dad," says Sam. She's built some fences, and has some horses and cows inside, along with a camel.

"Nice," says Paul. "Make sure they have enough room. You could build some more fences for them."

At that time of the morning, food comes quickly. For Sam, they've done toast soldiers with her eggs, where they actually cut out

44

legs and used those leftover parts to make arms, and put sultanas for eyes. She thinks that's pretty cool and eats the sultanas first.

Later that day we're heading to the park. Paul is wearing those footie shorts, ready for the promised game—not strictly promised, but he really seems to expect it, so I'll try to make sure it happens—and talking on his phone. It's on loudspeaker, and he passes it occasionally to Sam. I'm not listening in, but I do hear him called Fatty pretty constantly. I look at him again. He's really, really not fat.

At one point he's doing all the talking, so I ask Sam, "Why's he called Fatty?"

She shrugs. "Dunno. Some football thing. That's just Nan and Pop."

And I guess, ah, Paul "Fatty" Vautin. Former captain of the Queensland team, probably even around the time this Paul was born. I wonder if his parents are such huge rugby league fans that they named him after Vautin, or whether they just liked the name Paul and then the nickname followed. The maroon footie shorts, the team colours, are all of a piece with it.

When we get there, Sveta and Ted are already there with a picnic blanket and some supplies. Ted's drinking a beer, and Sveta a vodka mix.

"Is the sun over the yardarm yet?" I ask.

"Ages ago," says Ted.

Paul introduces Sam. He doesn't seem at all ill at ease with Sveta, despite what I think of as her brusqueness from their first meeting. And if there was any frostiness on her part, it's melted immediately. Even though Sveta says repeatedly she doesn't want kids of her own for a long time yet, she's pretty good with them. I've seen her at her sister's day care, when things have gotten a bit crazy as they do on occasion, help calm it all down.

Steve and Vijay wander along shortly afterwards, friends who'd often come and hang out at our house when we lived together; Steve's girlfriend and their kid—three years old now?—come too. Howie turns up last.

We sit around for a while, and everyone has one of their drink of choice, vodka or regular beer or low-carb beer for Howie. Then Howie tosses the football he brought up in the air and tells us it's time.

I'm not that much of a footie player. I'd play social games at uni, but it was Howie who was the regular player. I'd go and watch him sometimes, sitting on the sideline with a book and looking up occasionally, next to the girlfriend of the month; Sveta would be there too. She doesn't mind playing either, but she's not really built for it: her top half has to be pretty seriously strapped down. I don't think it is today, and while the rest of the guys might otherwise encourage her to play anyway, jokingly, they wouldn't with Ted there. Of the others, Steve is good, and Ted and Vijay are okay.

So we assign teams. Sveta is going to hang out with Steve's girlfriend and kid, and read *The Cat in the Hat* to Sam. I'm with Steve and Ted, and the other three are together. I don't know how good Paul is, but after the Fatty discovery and his conversation about footie that first evening with Howie, it could well be a talent of his.

And it is. He's fast and good at ducking and weaving, and definitely has ball skills. We're losing pretty badly, Steve and Ted and I. I don't mind losing—it's only friendly—but I don't want to be totally hopeless. So when I have my opportunity, I run with the ball towards our designated try line between a tree and a bin. I think I'll actually get us some points, finally, but I'm not fast enough. I'm tackled from behind, arms around my chest; we crash to the ground and I think I'm going to go face-first, nose into the dirt, but we twist at the last minute and most of the impact is taken by the shoulder of the body under me.

And I'm still being held. By Paul, the arms tell me. And the scent. I don't know whether it's objectively lasting for a long time, or whether it's my subjective experience of the skin of his legs against mine, the inner skin of his forearm against my belly where my shirt's ridden up, his breath against my neck, that make the seconds stretch out. And I start to get hard. I quickly look up to see if Sveta's watching—she's the one who'd be first to draw a conclusion here—but fortunately she's not, she's still reading, or reading again. I wriggle out of his grasp anyway, and lie on the ground for a bit, pretending to be winded, waiting until it's safe to get up.

Howie's jogging over, laughing. "We're playing touch, remember."

"This is how we play touch in Queensland." Paul grins and rubs the shoulder that he landed on. That we landed on.

"I think we should concede now and have another beer," I say to Steve and Ted. They don't put up any argument.

THE DAY just extends. We wander off home late afternoon, and Sam asks again about *Xena*, and I say she can come and watch the DVDs at my house. Paul has his palm behind his neck, elbow sticking up, in what I'm coming to characterize as his pondering pose.

"You could bring them over. Then I could make dinner later, and it would be easy to put Sam to bed."

"Whatever works for you."

So we do that. We watch two episodes—"That's Joxer," I say to Paul, several times—and with the third episode Paul goes to start cooking. I doze for maybe ten minutes—it's been a day of sun, fresh air, and beer—and wake up to a question from Sam.

"Who's that man with the beard?"

"That's Ares. He's the god of war. Not a good guy in this show."

"Okay. Does he like Xena?"

"Sort of." I think Sam's uncertain about this intrusion of romance, such as it is.

Then it's dinner and the usual routine—I think about how funny it is that it's become usual. Just talking about regular stuff. Paul mentions he's not sure what Sam will do for the summer—her regular day care is already booked up for the vacation since they arrived late in the year, and ex-Mrs Paul isn't committing to anything, although he phrases it in a more positive way with Sam sitting right there—and I tell him I might have an idea. Paul puts on a movie after Sam's in bed, a Bourne movie, and looks at me—is the choice okay? do I want to stay?—I'm not sure what the precise question is, but I nod and sit in the armchair.

This time Paul sits in Sam's beanbag, on the floor in front of me. We've watched about an hour of it, when his head rests on my leg. So there are a couple of possibilities here. The first is that this is what a guy in the closet might do. Especially after the footie incident. It's the kind of thing ex-boyfriend Trent did, the seemingly accidental bumps and touches from a supposed straight guy until I figured it out—we were young then, and clueless. Since then I've only been with guys who are out—serious Alexander and artistic Leo for two years each, crazy Gunther for a European working holiday romance of five months—so this is mostly outside my recent experience.

He hasn't moved while I've been considering this. And then his breathing starts turning to snores. Faint at first, the sound of a lip flap with each exhalation, then louder. That was the other possibility, which turns out to be the case without the necessity of further speculation by me: the sun, fresh air, and beer that had me dozing earlier, working on someone who usually goes to bed early anyway.

I sit there and keep watching the movie. He moves a couple of times, but doesn't fundamentally shift. My hands itch to run over his head, but I think to myself, *That's creepy*. It was justifiable in the fumbling relationship beginnings with Trent. I can look back at my younger self and not judge it too harshly, but now—terrible idea. Plus it would really get me hard. His hair's just the right length that brushing it at the back, up and down, with and then against the direction of growth, would go straight to my dick.

And I think to myself, *What kind of a sad individual have I become to be thinking this?* I acknowledge now that I like him more than I expected, that the liking has snuck up on me. But that doesn't justify my thoughts.

I suddenly have an image in my head from the movie *Maurice*. That's the movie where the quote came from about the unspeakable vice of the Greeks, I remember. The image is of Maurice the city professional with the gamekeeper Scudder in the boatshed, at the beginning of their implausible romance. I wonder if it's been bubbling away in my subconscious, and somehow started this ridiculous speculation of mine. Paul as Scudder.

I can live in the desert, I remind myself. I'm made for it.

The movie ends, and I move my leg so that Paul's head falls. He jerks up suddenly.

"Is it finished?" he asks, not sounding entirely with it.

"Yep. I think you fell asleep."

"Yeah, that happens. Sorry. Dull for you."

"No worries. I like it when guys fall asleep on me." Shit. Why did I say that? Just after I'd finished excoriating myself. It's the sort of thing I'd say to Axel or Howie, but I really shouldn't here. Still, he laughs. "On that note, I'll see myself out. G'night."

"G'night."

"Do you know," I ask Sveta, "if your sister has any places in her day care over the summer?"

I hear her brain ticking over in the silence. "Is this for your new neighbour?"

"Yeah. It seems like a tricky thing to arrange, especially having just moved to our neighbourhood. I remember John telling us about trying to get day care for his daughter." John was a casual friend from the house-sharing days. It was a very long description he gave us of the day-care search, almost Homeric in its dangers and problems; longer than I really thought was warranted, but I'd listened anyway, and Sveta and I had mimicked him gently afterwards. "Maybe you didn't really click with Paul, but I thought I'd help him out."

"I came along prepared for someone different, I suppose, that night I met him at Boney M. But he actually seems quite nice."

"Yeah, he's okay." A little positivity is okay, not too much. The tone is just right, I think.

"I'll ask Katarina, then."

"*Spasiba*."

She hangs up with a chuckle.

Then I get on and watch *Maurice*. My freak-out from last night has mostly receded, and rewatching this is to help bundle it up and push it away. It turns out the actual words of the line I like are "Omit:

a reference to the unspeakable vice of the Greeks." It's a while since I've seen the movie, and it's not quite as my memory has reconstructed it; which is good. I'm not really anything like Maurice, university graduate with a professional career though he is, with his lack of interest in books and for the most part lack of introspection, which if anything I tend to cripple myself with. "Mentally torpid," E.M. Forster calls him. And Paul isn't Scudder the gamekeeper. It's not just that the difference in class, so strongly situating the story in an England of a century ago, is so alien to us now; it's the book thing there, too, that Scudder is all physicality and not much interest in other things: he wouldn't want to talk about the *Iliad*. So it was just some superficial similarities that made me think of it last night, not that I'm somehow trying to recreate it in my life, and I'm feeling reassured. I'm just at the part near the end where they've met at the museum and Scudder is trying his blackmail in his working class, West Country accent— it's probably the point of the story where I'm least able to see myself in Maurice's shoes, still ready to love Scudder as he is—and I think, unlike Scudder, Paul would probably be interested in museums.

And I hear the clearing of a throat.

It's Paul, standing in the doorway of the room. Shit. I fumble for the remote, switch off the TV. Then I say to myself, *I'm not doing anything wrong; there's no need to look guilty*. He doesn't know what I was thinking about. I was just watching some random movie.

"Sorry," he says, "I called out at the front door, but I guess you didn't hear."

"Nah, I guess I zoned out a bit."

"Y'know, walking into someone's house is just what we'd do if they didn't hear us from the veranda. You looked a bit startled. Maybe it's not a city thing."

"It's fine. It's probably not something we do here, but you're fine to do it. As I said, I was just a bit out of it."

"Anyway, I just came over because I hoped I could borrow some tinned tomatoes. I've already done the groceries with Sam today and forgot to get them then, and I thought it would be easier than taking her out again. Less crankiness at bedtime."

"Sure." I get two tins from the kitchen and bring them back for him.

"Ta. I didn't mean to interrupt your movie. You can go back to watching it now."

"Nah, wasn't anything much."

My heart slows as he leaves.

It's Thursday night, and I'm over at Paul and Sam's again for dinner. This time they asked specifically since I'll be leaving tomorrow. Sam wants to watch another episode of *Xena*, so we do. I left early from work and have already packed, so I'm pretty relaxed.

This evening, it's spaghetti marinara.

"What's this?" asks Sam, pointing.

"A prawn," says Paul.

She eats it, and it seems to pass the five-year-old palate test. "What's this?"

"Octopus."

"Octopus? Eww."

"Ohmigod," I say, "that's its tentacle. It could attack me." I fish it out—fortunately it's fairly free of the tomato sauce—and move it towards my face. "Ohmigod, it is attacking me." I press it against my cheek. "Argh, it's got me! I've got to eat it to save myself." I chomp it down, quickly.

"That's really dumb," says Sam. But she eats a tentacle too.

"We don't play with our food here," says Paul, but he's smiling.

After dinner and kid bedtime, Paul goes to put on a movie. "Do you have to leave early?"

"I'm all organized, so a movie sounds good."

"Okay. I got *Wrath of the Titans*, since you like *Xena* and the *Iliad* and stuff."

So we watch it, back to the usual sofa and armchair combination. We're probably an hour into it and Paul says, "This is really bad. I'm sorry. Let's just switch it off."

"Nah, it's fine," I say, even though it's true that it's not a great movie.

"Really, we should switch it off, it's so bad."

I have the remote. I'm torn. It's true it is his house and his TV and his remote. But if I don't see the end of the movie, it will bug me for the whole flight tomorrow. And if it's not showing on the flight, I'll have to rent it when I get to LA. "I have to finish watching it, it's just a thing." So I hold the remote away from him. He laughs, and gets up, and I get up, and we scuffle and jump and get turned around and he lunges, and I fall backwards on the sofa and he falls on top of me, reaching up to grip my arms although still not getting the remote.

This time I'm sure that it's lasting an objectively long time.

"You're lying on me," I say after a while.

"Yeah," he says. He doesn't move.

I move my right leg up between his two legs, naked as they are up to his shorts, feel the touch of the hair there. He still doesn't move.

I lean my head up and kiss him.

He mashes his face against mine and moves his arms down to grip me so tightly it's hard to breathe, so I grip him back the same way, and he laughs, a small puff of surprise or disbelief. We almost roll off the sofa, and he says, "Shh, sleeping kid." So I think that will be the end of it, but instead, he pulls me up by the arm and leads me to his room.

WHEN WE'RE in his room, he says, "I'm new at this."

I smile. "Arms up." He does, and I pull his T-shirt over his head. "Shorts off too?" He nods, so I pull them down, running my fingers down the insides of his thighs as I do. When they're at his ankles, he kicks them to the corner of the room. I flop back on his bed, propped up on my elbows, and look at him. His chest is leanly muscled and lightly haired, the hair mostly on the lower half of his pecs and then leading in a thin trail down to his belly button, and then fanning out; his legs are more heavily haired, which I've seen a lot of before already, courtesy of the footie shorts. His briefs are old, the elastic partly gone around the waist. His cock is pointing up and to the right, and the loose elastic lets me see just the tip of the head. "You are ridiculously hot."

He laughs and launches himself on me. My T-shirt and shorts come off too, and briefs as well, and then he grabs me in a full-body grasp as tight as before, so almost all of our skin is touching, only his briefs still in the way. The sensation: it's like going from drought to flood in ten seconds. I feel his cock start to poke into my belly, so I reach down with my hands to pull down his briefs, then use my feet to drag them off the rest of the way. He's still holding me really tight. I insert my hand between us and grip our cocks together. I still haven't seen his fully yet, but it feels about the same size as mine, maybe thicker. His grip gets even tighter, and he starts grinding. All I need to do is hold us together, and soon he's shooting between us. My face is in his neck; when I feel him shudder, I come too.

WE'RE LYING on his bed. I'm on my back; he's on his side, one elbow bent, his head resting on his hand, facing me. I'm looking at his legs: one thigh has a large freckle, and his cock is snaking along that thigh. His stomach is tight but not ostentatiously six-packed; there are another two freckles on his right side. On the arm that's propping up his head, the bicep looks like there's a small football under the skin, and along his wrist, the veins are so prominent and so blue they look like a river delta.

"Am I Scudder?" he asks.

"How—" I'm at a loss for words. "No. You're too thoughtful. And I'm not Maurice." I think for a bit. "How do you even know about Scudder?"

He grins. "There's this thing called Google, and you can find out lots of stuff using it." I open my mouth to say something. "On Sunday when I wandered into your house, and you flicked off the movie, you looked so freaked out. Like I'd caught you wanking. Which I wouldn't have minded, by the way. But I saw the DVD case, so I did some detective work. Fortunately the local movie rental place had a copy."

"And this is why you're not Scudder. He was good at climbing up to first-floor windows, not so good at detective work." I clear my throat. "I was just watching it because I thought I was fooling myself into thinking you were interested out of some literary fantasy. Misinterpreting things like your footie tackle."

"Actually, you didn't misinterpret that. But you didn't react, and even when you said that thing about liking guys falling asleep on you, I couldn't tell whether it meant you were interested. Too cool, you were." He pauses, looking me over. "Even though you're kind of skinny, you've definitely got some muscle. Your legs especially." It's true I don't put on muscle that easily, and have to make sure not to miss time at the gym; the legs just come from all the cycling. "I like the way it feels I won't break you."

I look at him for a moment. "Can I do something?"

He looks wary. "What?"

"Nothing serious." I sit up, lean over, hold on to his hip, and kiss the jaw muscle I've been wanting to kiss since I saw it, then continue on down to his chin. "I really wanted to kiss your jaw. I'm not cool."

He laughs. When I look down, he's fully hard again. With my left hand I wipe up some of the come that's pooled on my stomach, slightly congealed but still serviceable; with my right hand I push his shoulders onto the bed, and stroke the come along his cock. He gives a full-body shudder, but I keep stroking. His legs twitch and his neck muscles strain as he tilts his head back: it's not that long since we came, so he's undoubtedly still a bit sensitive, but he doesn't seem to mind. It takes longer this time, and the gasp at the end is intense.

CHAPTER 5

BACK IN my bed that night, I lie awake. Paul seemed okay when I left, no freak-out on his part, not like the way Trent was all those years ago, the foreshadowing of how it would all end badly. But it might be a different story in the morning. I'd told him that I wouldn't tell anyone, that I understood how it is, but that might not be enough to reassure him. In hindsight, if this had been a purely rational, thoroughly planned operation, it wouldn't have taken place the night before I was going overseas and unable to influence what happens next, smooth over anything that needs it. Unable even to know what's going on.

So I get little sleep. My flight's mid-morning, and I have to leave for the airport relatively early. That means I'm up already while he's getting ready for work and getting Sam ready for day care. I knock on his door. It seems like a long time before he answers, but he does. "I thought you might need some more tomatoes," I say, holding out a tin. "You used them up last night."

He looks slightly quizzical, but otherwise normal. "Thanks." No sign of freaking out, of avoiding me. "I wasn't sure what time you were leaving and whether I'd see you. I hope your trip's good." He holds out a hand to shake. Maybe that's just what you do in Queensland the morning after; so I shake. He holds my hand for longer than usual, and then runs his thumb over the back of my hand, back and forth. I smile, and he smiles back, even more broadly. "Come back soon."

I'M IN luck, sort of, that the flight does have *Wrath of the Titans* among its selection of eight hundred movies, so I can watch the end of it and satisfy my completionist urges. It doesn't take my mind off Paul and the situation with him, which in spite of the positive farewell, I'm still worrying about. It's a long flight to LA, a long time for reflection to lead to a change of heart.

Worrying notwithstanding, the flight's a pretty normal one, and as usual I'm operating at about 80 percent when I get off the plane. There's the usual shuffling queue, the usual wait at immigration, and I switch on my phone to browse news and weather. That's when I see there's a message from Paul. I open it: it's a picture of Rupert Graves, who played Scudder in the movie, and I laugh. I find a stock image of James Wilby—Maurice—and send that back. When I get to the immigration desk, I'm quizzed for longer than usual about my purpose in visiting the US. Maybe looking happy is suspicious.

MONDAY ISN'T awkward, even though I see Xavier first thing when I get into the LA Fire Department headquarters where we're doing our work. It's true that it was a minor blow to the ego, being dumped, but I've already had my wallowing in melancholy, and it's not as if it were some deep connection that had been severed. He seems a bit uncertain—not super obvious, I don't think the other guys here notice anything—so I go and shake his hand, along with everyone else's. "Welcome back," says Chris, someone else I've worked closely with here. Not as closely as with Xavier, of course.

The morning is some meetings—not with hunky firemen, but with administrative types. We talk about what they want: things like being able to access information on where hazardous waste is stored, and maybe by cross-referencing this with data held by the Environmental Protection Agency, they could find out undeclared hazards. I point out some potential privacy issues—even though no one this time suggests I "just hack into" the EPA and "just get the damn data," they're keen for some more legal version of that to happen—and I get to do the demo I'd prepared to explain what's feasible and what's not. My role here isn't so much programming, more sorting out what people really want versus what can be done. The company refers to me when I'm doing that as a forward deployed embeddee. Hah. Who comes up with these names?

THE SPARKY

When we break for lunch, on the way to the cafeteria, I send Paul a picture I'd taken of the front of the LAFD building with its eagle logo, captioned "my work today." It's only a short while later, when I'm in the queue for a sandwich, that he sends back a photo of his tool belt, also captioned "my work today." I type "Hot toolkit"—think, *That's really cringeworthy, delete it*—type it again, think, *Maybe it is cringeworthy but it'll help me gauge from over here how comfortable he's feeling about things*—press send. I'm sitting down at a table with Xavier and Chris and some others when I get a reply. It's just a photo of Paul's hand gripping a screwdriver upside down, one thumb in the midst of caressing the rounded handle head. I stifle a laugh.

Xavier's sitting next to me. I can tell he wants to say something, so I put the phone away and look at him, giving him a nod.

"How are things?" he asks.

"All good." I want to assure him that it's all fine, and at the same time that we don't have to talk about it. It wasn't really enough of a thing, what we'd had going. Also, we're at the lunch table—even if it had been enough of a thing, I wouldn't want to get into it here.

"I wasn't sure—"

"Really, all good." I smile. He's wearing his usual form-fitting business shirt and trousers, which are flattering but aren't doing anything for me. If I were still feeling melancholy, it might be a different story, but it's surprising how quickly I was over that.

"Maybe we could catch up one evening."

I'm ambivalent, but—"Yeah, okay."

IT'S MY last day, and Xavier and I are going out. Things have been going fine, much the same as since I arrived. Xavier's gradually returned to normal, and even jokes around a little. I don't mind.

I go back to my hotel room and get changed into the one going-out outfit I've brought with me, a short-sleeved black shirt and jeans, plain but well-tailored. We're going somewhere in West Hollywood, so it should blend in okay. I don't really have any kind of coat that goes with the shirt—didn't think that through completely when packing—and it is cold outside, so I decide that just this once I'll get some alcohol from the minibar to help keep me warm in case I'm out of doors at all. There's a miniature whiskey, so I pour that into a glass and sip it.

Xavier arrives in a cab, and I go downstairs and jump in. "You look good," he says. It could just be politeness, but his eyes do linger on my arms for a second.

"You too." He does, but unsurprisingly I'm still not feeling it: mine is just a polite comment.

We go to the Abbey. It is a bit touristy, but there are locals too; and I am a sort of tourist anyway, and haven't been here before. But it's won an award for best gay bar in the world, Xavier had said to me, as if that meant I should have made it my first destination on my first trip to LA. Won twice, he'd said. There's a queue at the door, not too long, although I'm glad of the earlier whiskey for the warmth.

We get a table and give our order to Ben. I'm over here often enough that the familiarity of the waiters—"Hi, I'm Ben, and I'll be your server for this evening," in his case with a wink to complement his tight T-shirt—so forced-seeming compared to home, doesn't seem totally unnatural the way it did at first. When he comes back with a mojito for each of us, Xavier thanks him with a wide smile, and then has second thoughts and looks at me. Of course I was expecting him to flirt when we came here—it's like breathing for him—so I shake my head and smile.

The music's loud, but we still manage to talk a bit. He's planning to move house soon, probably somewhere near here, and is weighing up possible places to live. Then he wants to dance. Dancing isn't really my thing, but I get up anyway, and we thread our way through crowds surrounding some go-go boys and girls. After about ten minutes Xavier has his shirt off and it's hanging from his back pocket: he's really getting into the music. He looks at me and I smile. He seems fully present, gaze intense; I'm thinking of *Xena* and *Wrath of the Titans* and screwdrivers, and the texts that have continued throughout my time in LA. I'm not making too much of our interactions, Paul's and mine—I'm not, really, it would be ridiculous to make too much out of a handful of texts and one-time sex that might come to be a source of regret—but I'd rather be back there.

Xavier goes to put his arms around my neck so we're dancing together, but that's the point at which a guy comes along. Also shirtless, pretty sweaty so he's probably been dancing awhile. He puts his hands on both of our shoulders and raises his eyebrows. It's an invitation for something. Xavier looks at him: he's drunk and danced enough that he doesn't show the same hesitation about offending me that he has up until now.

"I'm going," I say into his ear. "My flight's pretty early tomorrow." He looks torn. I kiss him on the cheek. "You stay." I thread my way out. He doesn't follow.

I'M BACK late on Sunday, then into work on Monday. Everything's gone well, so it's fine for me to leave relatively early. I'm in time for dinner next door. Paul hasn't actually invited me, and in fact doesn't actually know I'm back today, but I figure I can just drop past and be guaranteed that he and Sam are still awake. It's partly just checking that things are okay—there was a vibe of okayness coming across in our texts, but face to face could be a different story.

I do check that I look decent before I go next door and knock on the door.

Paul opens it, and his smile is broad. It feels face-to-face okay, even without saying anything. Sam comes to the door too. "Hi, Aaron," she says.

"Hi, Sam. I brought you back something from America." I pull the *Scooby-Doo* Lego from behind my back. "It says it's for age six and older, so it might be a bit tricky, but we can help you do it if you want."

She starts happily shaking the box. "That's awesome! Can we do it now?"

"Well, I hadn't told your dad I'd be here today, so he's not really expecting me, and I'm guessing you're about to have dinner." I look at Paul while I'm speaking.

"No worries. I'll just chuck in more spaghetti."

"As long as you don't mind."

"I don't mind." His smile's either saying that I sound ridiculously formal, or that he's hoping for something. Maybe both.

Sam and I manage to assemble about half of the Mystery Machine before dinner is served. Paul talks about jobs he's been doing around the neighbourhood—he seems to have been getting more of them, which is good—and I read between the lines of a couple of his comments about a repeat customer who comes to the door wearing a negligee.

"What's a negligee?" asks Sam.

"Her pyjamas," says Paul. "I guess she's a sleepyhead."

Sam's news is about her friend Bec and how they did some painting today, and she painted a horse, and Bec painted a doll. For my news—it's become the pattern, really, having dinner here and talking about what we've been doing, and this is my catching up after a gap of a couple of weeks—I open my phone's photo gallery and pass it to Sam.

"Hey, that's you! And he's old now!"

Paul has a quizzical look on his face.

"Pass it to your dad," I say.

He takes the phone, pauses a second. "Joxer." He smiles. I like how much he's been smiling this evening.

"Yep. Ted Raimi is the actor. He was at a fan convention the middle weekend I was there, so I couldn't resist."

There's been some music playing in the background, which I hadn't really noticed, apart from a vague awareness that I liked it, some typical Australian rock.

"Do you like Hunters and Collectors?" Paul asks. That's who's playing. Right now it's a song I know, one of their most famous. "Throw Your Arms Around Me." It's at the chorus now, exhorting me to shed my skin and get started.

I smile. "I do."

After parallel washing up and bedtime, Paul comes into the kitchen. "I don't know if you feel like hanging around. Maybe watch some TV." He pauses. "Sam's usually awake for another half an hour."

"I accept your invitation." Both of them.

He gets two beers and we head into the TV room. He sits on the sofa as usual. I stay standing for a moment, and then take off my shirt. He looks slightly alarmed.

"After Los Angeles, it's really warm here. Just getting comfortable." I can't help laughing with the corniness. It should come with a bow-chicka-wow-wow and cheesy electronic music. He laughs too, but the nervousness is still there. Then instead of sitting in the chair I sit at the other end of the sofa, and put my legs up. I can touch his leg with the sole of my foot, and I do. "And I'm tired from jetlag, so I'm lying on this lounge."

He looks like he doesn't quite know what to do. Get up and move to the chair? Sit in the beanbag?

"Come on, I'll just sit here," I say. "Lie here. Nothing else. I've given you a story that'll sound plausible to a five-year-old. I just want to—" I touch his leg again with my foot. "—do that. What are we going to watch?"

It could be a documentary about canola that he's switched on. Or maybe about sheep. Paul keeps glancing at me, at my chest. That's a nice feeling—you wonder with guys of ambiguous sexuality whether they just enjoyed you getting them off, or whether they're actually attracted to you. He seems to want to look at my chest, even though I'm remembering his description of me as skinny. And after a while, at a point when a shearer is being interviewed on the TV, he puts his hand on the foot of mine near him, fingers between the toes. That feels even nicer.

"Put your legs up on the sofa too," I say. "I'm sure you're tired after working today. All that work with customers in negligees."

He hesitates but puts his legs up on the sofa too. My one leg is between the two of his. I do what he's been doing, lacing my fingers between his toes, then press the soles of his feet, pushing the thumb in, the way I like it myself. His head tilts back a little. And then I can't resist, and I press my foot into his crotch. He inhales, but doesn't move. I apply pressure, gently, move my foot around. I can feel him getting hard. Harder. Harder still.

"Stop," he says. I stop. He takes a few deep breaths. "I'll see if Sam is asleep." He gets up and his shorts are really tented out.

When he comes back, he nods. "Asleep." He's still hard. I put out a hand and he pulls me up from the sofa. It's a little more forceful than necessary, so I pretend-stumble into him. He grabs me around the waist. "Stay a bit longer?" he asks.

"For sure." I hum the chorus of "Throw Your Arms Around Me." We head into his bedroom, and he's just as keen as the first time.

AFTER, I say to him, "You said you're new to this, but you're not as—hesitant as I'd expected. I know of guys who took months to get to this point." Know guys. Trent.

Paul shrugs. "It's like this is a whole separate world here. Different. Anything goes." Anything doesn't go, of course, but I can kind of see the perspective. From Central Queensland it must seem like an all-you-can-eat buffet of decadence.

"You know, I thought you were warning me off, telling me about your brother-in-law that time."

"Nah, not at all. It was that he came on to me while I was going out with Kaylee. That was the thing. I said you weren't like him. Even if I hadn't been going out with Kaylee, I'd never have thought of doing anything with him. Not like with you."

He puts his arms around me and holds me from behind.

CHAPTER 6

TUESDAY AND Wednesday, I'm unreasonably frustrated by not being able to leave work early. There's some pair programming, which, by definition, I can't leave to be done solo, and I get home after everything's dark next door. I feel like a teenager, at the mercy of hormones or feelings or both; tell myself it's silly; don't feel any differently after the self-remonstration.

Thursday afternoon, when a meeting looks likely to arise, I pretend to be sick. The thought of the proposed meeting does strike at my gut like a cudgel of blahness. Have I ever done this before, getting out of something by pretending to be sick rather than manning up and just doing it? Maybe when I was in high school.

I make it in time for dinner next door, with its miraculous curative properties.

"Aaron!" says Sam as I walk through the door. "Can you help me finish this?"

There's been a little progress on Lego *Scooby-Doo*, but it's not done yet. "Sure." I call out a hello to Paul in the kitchen.

A little later we're finishing it up, and Paul's watching as Sam drives the Mystery Machine around with Shaggy on the roof. "Dinner's ready when you guys are."

"We are."

While we're eating, Paul takes advantage of a pause in Sam's chatter to make a request. "So all those books you read—any suggestions for me? I used to read more, but, y'know. Life."

I wonder what he might like. I know that he knows *Lord of the Rings*, and has made his way through the *Iliad*, all unprompted. So I shouldn't shy away from a challenging read, but it'd be good if it's something that will speak to him. Maybe something Australian. I tell him I'll think about it.

After the bedtime routine, tonight Paul suggests we sit out the back. The sun's just about set, but he has a new light installed above the back door that illuminates the whole yard. He's a little longer than I expected in bringing out the beers. When he comes out the door, he's not wearing a shirt, just the footie shorts. I wonder if it's just the single pair of those Queensland footie shorts he has, or whether he has multiple identical ones.

"Warm," he says as he sits in the chair. I laugh.

I grumble a bit about work, stuff that was too boring for a five-year-old at dinner. Not saying to Paul that it's bad—it isn't—just that sometimes I wish I could get away. I skirt around why I want to get away, what I want to be doing instead—not just the sex, but spending time here. It all feels too tentative to make that kind of admission.

As I'm talking, he bends a leg and puts one of his feet up on his chair, resting his beer on a knee. My grumbling grinds to a halt as his cock falls out of the other leg of the shorts. I stare at it—I distantly think that it's like snake charming, except here the snake is hypnotizing me—as it lengthens along his thigh.

He breaks what's turned into a silence. "So do you do—other stuff?"

I think I can successfully narrow this description to something to do with sex, but nothing more specific than that. S&M? I hope not. "What kind of other stuff?"

"Like, blow jobs."

I smile, just a small smile, and don't say "duh." I put my beer down and get out of my chair, kneel down in front of him, put my hands on his legs. He breathes in.

"You can take your shirt off," he says.

"Should I?"

"Yeah."

So I take off my shirt and then his shorts, Paul lifting his hips so I can slide them down his legs. When I ease his cock out of the leg of the shorts—no underwear—it flicks up against his belly. I reach over for my beer and take another swallow to wet my lips, kneel up so I'm over the top of his cock, and then take the head in my mouth. He breathes in, sharper than before.

As I run my tongue around the rim of the head, I slide my hands up his thighs, the inside that's often sensitive. It is for him too: he bucks in the chair, pushing himself farther into my mouth. I go a little farther still, and then let his cock slip out from between my lips.

"Can you get out—your dick too?" He swallows.

I take off my shorts, put my shorts under my knees, stroke myself a little. I'm already hard.

"Do you mind doing this?" he asks.

"Are you kidding?" I point to my cock.

He gives a short laugh. "I guess not."

He watches as I stroke myself a couple more times, and then I block his view as I go down on him again. He seems taken by surprise, and with his surprise comes his ejaculation. I finish myself off—I was close—as I'm swallowing. Some escapes from my mouth and lands on his leg.

We sit there naked for a while. "Kaylee said once she thought I was gay. It was one time we were fighting."

"What did you say?"

"Nothing. I was close to breaking something—the fight had been going on for a while in those loud whispers you do—but Sam was asleep, so I just left. Drove around for a while. It was always like that. Sometimes it was that our car was crap and we should have a better one, or we should live in the city. Brisbane, she meant, but it was part of the reason we came here. There was always something wrong."

"Maybe she was trying to find something to blame you for, some reason to end it."

He shrugs. "I didn't know what she'd come out with sometimes. The gay thing—clearly, she just pulled that one out of nowhere. I had married her after all."

Clearly. I watch as a drip of come falls from his leg to the ground. Is this a good time to have a discussion about this? About whether he sees himself as gay, or bi, or maybe not-gay-just-messing-around? I don't think so. I think of Trent, so firmly in that last category. It's been a good night, and I don't feel like that conversation.

"HI, DEELIE."

"Hi, Aaron. You know, only you call me that now."

"Okay, Cordelia." There's some murmuring in the background, but it gets fainter—I guess she was with friends and is moving to where she can hear me better on the phone. My sister's at boarding school—our parents have always had jobs that take them around the world, so they figured that boarding school was the best thing for her. She has mixed feelings about it, but on the whole thinks it's a decent place.

"I don't mind or anything," she says.

"How are things?" There's silence. "Are you shrugging?" Talking to Deelie on the phone can be cryptic.

"Yeah. Things are okay." Then her voice gets muffled, but I can still hear her calling out to her friends. "It's my brother. I'm going to get a milkshake. Back in ten minutes."

I decide to go for a milkshake too, from the small milk bar on the corner of the local park. We talk as we walk.

"Things better with Danielle?" Danielle was her BFF until last term. I don't completely understand what happened—I think Danielle was more friendly with a new girl who arrived, and Deelie felt left out—but Deelie was pretty upset about it for weeks, in the way only teenagers can be. I was an intense teenager too, I guess, although it's a long time ago now. And friends had told me from when Deelie was a preteen that it was worse for girls, with the way group dynamics work, so when she was ten I watched *Mean Girls* to get prepared. That only scratched the surface.

"Sort of." That's the most positive thing she's said for a long time. "We hang out with friends at different times, and I've been hanging out more with my art friends." But no more making sure to be at opposite ends of the school grounds at all times, it sounds like.

"Hey, speaking of art, did anything arrive from me?"

"Oh, yeah, thanks. That was actually pretty cool." It was a reproduction of daguerreotype from the Getty in LA, a portrait of a woman from the 1840s, sitting in a chair. She's quite beautiful—her dark hair's pulled back in a simple style, and if you ignore the black ruffled dress, she'd still be considered a stunner today. I thought Deelie would appreciate the artistry behind the shot, as well as the look. I could see her doing that hairstyle. "The picture of you with Joxer, though, was really daggy. When I come and live with you, my room will be a nerd-free zone."

I laugh. "I'll try to tone it down, then." We reach our milkshake-purchasing venues at about the same time, and both order caramel. I sit on one of the collection of odd chairs that looks out onto the park.

"You'll be there at Christmas, right?" she asks.

"Yep. Only a few weeks away now. You know that when I come down there, we'll be going to see the new Star Wars together, young padawan."

"Yes, Obi Wan." I hear the grin in her voice for a split second before the scorn mandated by adolescence kicks in. "I mean, whatever, you dork." She mocks me, but she can quote lines from all the first six movies.

She sounds quite upbeat for the rest of the conversation.

IT'S A Saturday morning, and I'm looking after Sam. It's a little stressful—it's the first time I'm looking after her by myself, apart from that emergency visit to the hardware store by Paul; plus I'm organizing a barbecue-reunion thing for uni friends this afternoon, after having been thinking for a while about how much I used to enjoy everyone just hanging out at our house, the house where Howie and I used to live. But I was already mostly organised, so when Paul got a call last night to beg him to do some urgent electrical work this morning, and he asked me if I could mind Sam, I figured I could still fit it all in. Howie agrees to help out by picking up some of the drinks.

We go to the park first, and then go for a milkshake; Sam chooses strawberry, I have my usual caramel along with an espresso. We follow that up with a trip to the bookshop to get her a new book.

After that we walk along the main street until we reach my goal, the cat rescue society. The bell jingles as we go through the door, and a young woman with dyed black hair and three lip rings comes out from behind the back. "Can I help you?"

"Yeah, I expect I'll need some help in a minute. We'll just look at the cats for a bit first." Sam is already squatting down on her haunches, saying hello to the first cat, a grey-and-white one, in a voice that seems to be her reimagining of how adults talk to babies.

"Hello, kitty," she says with her singsong intonation, "you look like a nice kitty."

After squatting down with her I get back up to talk to the woman. "So I'm looking for a cat that's good with kids, just for indoors, and that's happy to be alone sometimes."

"All cats are happy to be alone sometimes," she says. That may be a small smile that accompanies her words; surely a sneer is out of place. Although this isn't a conventional shop, and the people who work here are volunteers. Maybe she's just unpractised with smiling.

"So which ones do you think might suit?"

She does know her cats, and makes a number of suggestions that we winnow down to three.

"Hey, Sam, c'mover here for a sec." She stops talking to the cats and comes over. "I want you to tell me which one's your favourite out of these cats."

She squats down again to begin new conversations with our three candidates. One of them, the youngest one, is a gingerish tabby; it jumps up against the glass of its enclosure and bats a paw against it a few times.

"This one," says Sam.

Paying for everything takes another few minutes. "I'll take it home tomorrow," I tell the goth girl.

"Her," she corrects me.

"Her," I repeat.

WHEN WE get back Paul's already there.

"How was it?" he asks.

"Piece of cake. Park, milkshake, walk along the street."

"I really appreciate it, mate."

"No worries at all. It was fun." Sam's gone inside. "There was one thing…."

"Yeah?"

"I'm planning to get a cat."

"A cat? Why? We'd shoot cats on the farm."

"Well, don't shoot this one. A reason I hadn't got one before is that I travel a lot. Don't say anything yet," I say, forestalling the awareness I see dawning on his face. "There are food dispensers that'll sort out the feeding for a couple of weeks, and Howie has said he can come over and look in on her occasionally. He doesn't really like his current housemates, so he might even stay over sometimes; I'm pretty sure it won't be a hassle for him. Anyway, you won't have to do much."

"Her?" He spots the pronoun.

"So maybe I've already picked one. I'd thought that maybe Sam could help look after the cat too. Not too much involved in it. It'd just be coming over sometimes and filling up the water bowl and stuff."

"Yeah, okay."

"And you just have to promise not to shoot her."

"Okay." He smiles. "What's her name?"

"We looked at a few of them this morning, Sam and I. I thought I'd get Sam to give her a name. Cats never pay attention to their name anyway, so it can be whatever. Now, second favour: could you help me set up for the house party today? You and Sam can still come, right? Other kids for Sam to play with and all."

"Sure thing."

HALF AN hour before people are supposed to arrive, we're ready. Howie and Sveta have come over to help too; Ted's doing some work thing, but should be here later. Ice and drinks are in the bathtub; meat patties and some chickpea alternatives are in the esky near the barbecue; onions and bread are sliced; furniture's been moved around so anyone who wants to can watch the cricket. A difference from the house parties of uni days is the bouncy castle out the back for kids of the friends who are now parents: that's just been inflated. So while Sam's watching a *Scooby-Doo* video, we're standing around in the kitchen, with three beers and a vodka, relaxed.

"The old organizational skills are still there," says Howie. He seems really up; remembering how much he used to enjoy these. He has a more sophisticated life now, with journalism and modelling, and probably much wilder times, but this is the thing that appealed to the country boy in him. Still does apparently. "Aaron used to do most of it when we lived together," he says to Paul. "Planning, planning, planning."

"Do you remember when he came out to us?" asks Sveta.

"God, no," I groan.

"Of course! But I'm guessing Paul doesn't know."

Paul shakes his head with a smile.

"So it was just before a party—" says Sveta.

"And he had these *palm cards*—" interjects Howie.

"He'd rehearsed—"

"And actually made palm cards, and he started reading from them—"

"I wasn't reading from palm cards." I'd only looked at them occasionally so I wouldn't freeze. I've put my beer down and have my hands over my face, so my voice is probably muffled. I don't usually mind the story—I've made it an anecdote myself, told it at my own expense—but I'm finding it embarrassing today.

"You were!" says Howie, and they proceed to tell the rest of the story, Howie's declaration that I was the first gay guy he'd met, and Sveta's hefting up of her breasts to confirm that they weren't my thing, although she had already noted my lack of interest in them.

Paul's laughing. And then he says, "And do you know how he came out to me?"

Howie's gaze goes wide. "No, how?"

Sveta asks me, "Why haven't you told us?"

Paul looks at me and I shrug in resignation. "So I've just made a mess of my kitchen—it's like the one we're standing in here, but lots of work to be done on it—and I need to rush out to Reece for supplies to fix my stuff-up, and taking Sam would have been hard, eh. I'm standing on the front step asking Aaron a favour, if he can just mind Sam for ten minutes, blood gushing from my arm where I've cut it on this rusty metal"—I roll my eyes at the exaggeration and he smiles broadly—"and he says, 'I'm gay.'"

Howie and Sveta have almost identical incredulous expressions on their faces. "What?"

"In my defence," I say, "it does make sense." So I explain—having had some time, I've thought about how not to call Paul a yokel in doing so—and finish with, "I have realized how dorky it sounded." Howie and Sveta are laughing.

"Nah, you're cool," says Paul.

"I'm not cool," I say, smiling.

He runs his hand along his jaw and smiles back.

ABOUT THIRTY people turn up. That makes it a little tightly packed into my house, but it's cosy rather than claustrophobic, just the casual catch-up I'd imagined and wanted to recreate from uni days. There are a few here that I don't know—it was an open invitation for bringing people along—but most are friends from uni. All older, most slightly heavier, but it's good to see them again. There's a knot of them settled in, in front of the cricket, another group in the backyard near the bouncy castle watching over the kids—six kids altogether, including Sam—and random whorls and eddies of other people catching up and then moving on to the next remembered face.

Paul doesn't stick at my side, as I'd wondered if he might. Even when I'm in conversations, I notice where he is—he does a lot of the barbecuing, which is helpful; he chats to Howie; he takes a turn monitoring the castle; surprisingly, he spends quite a lot of time with

Sveta, who is still sans Ted. Howie seems to have latched on to a dark-haired girl that I don't know, a friend of a friend I assume.

I'm talking to Isabella when Paul comes over. I used to spend a lot of time with Isabella at uni, drinking black coffee and arguing about books and politics. Since then there's only been the occasional comment on Facebook between us to recall it, to bring back the feeling of friendship we'd had, but now in person we've fallen back into it as if it were only a semester ago rather than the best part of a decade.

"So what are you reading now?" she's asking.

"*An Open Swimmer*," I say. I nod to Paul. "This is Paul, who lives next door. He's reading it too."

"Are you part of a book club?"

"Sort of."

"What do you think of it?"

"I'm having a bit of trouble getting into Jerra's head," I say. He's the teenage protagonist, not too long out of school; I often don't understand his motivations, something that's complicated by the patches of dialogue that are unattributed and paragraph fragments that are scattered randomly and have to be pieced together to work out what happened when Jerra was younger.

"I had trouble with the old man and what he did," Isabella says. It turns out the old man killed his wife by burning down their beach shack around her. I guess Isabella's trying to avoid a spoiler here, although Paul and I are both up to that part. Isabella turns her attention to Paul. "What do you think of it?"

Paul's silent for a moment. "The way he talks about water is—it makes you know it, eh. I've never been to the beach, but now it feels like I have. Jerra and Sean camping, too, that's all real, just the way camping is. I figure I don't have to understand everything Jerra does." He's not looking at either of us.

Isabella, however, is looking at him: I think she'd dismissed him at first as a handsome face she couldn't possibly be interested in, but now suddenly she sees depths that make him worth paying attention to. Her posture changes to signal her interest, chin and shoulders and hips. "I know what you mean about the descriptions of the ocean. Tim Winton really is an amazing writer." *Back off sister,* I think, half joking.

"You've never been to the beach?" I ask.

"Nah, not swimming. Holidays as a kid were all camping. It's a bit far from inland Queensland to the beach. And then when I was grown up Sam was small, and that made it hard too. Now that she's five, but, it might be easier." The mention of a kid and the spectre of an associated wife seem to register with Isabella, and her posture returns to what it was before her brief, and probably unrecognized by its target, moment of flirtatiousness.

It's 8.00 p.m., and we're just tidying up, Howie and Sveta and I. Howie's wittering on about Mandy, the dark-haired girl he spent a lot of time talking to. She's a backpacker from Ireland, the western part, near the island where those sweaters are made, and did I know that they actually speak Irish there mostly, rather than just English as in most of the country? I nod at appropriate points. A country girl from the other side of the world. Sveta's more quiet; I wonder if it has anything to do with Ted not showing. I'd expected him to, once whatever work thing he was doing was over.

Paul comes back in the front door then. "Sorry I missed most of the cleanup. I told Sam I was just coming back here to help, and if she wakes up she'll know where I am."

"We're doing okay," I say. "If you'd rather not leave her, we'll handle it here." We're not too far from being done anyway.

"Nah, she's fine. All that jumping on the castle, there's no chance she'll wake up. She was already sound asleep when I left."

So we pick up the remaining cans and bottles, nearly filling Paul's recycling bin as well as mine. There's enough for two loads of the dishwasher; I get one going, and leave the rest for later.

"That was an excellent idea," says Howie as he gets ready to go. "We should do it again." Sveta, a little more muted, agrees. "Are you catching the train?" he asks her, and she nods. "Me too. Walk you to the station." And they head out the door.

As they leave, I lean back against the kitchen bench. It was fun, but there's always the tenseness that comes with organizing it all, making sure things go the way they should, and the draining away of that tension is almost as good in its own way as the fun of the event itself.

"That was pretty good. Sam had a ball," says Paul. "You want to come over for a bit to relax?"

I look at him. "Yeah, that'd be nice."

When we get to his place he sits at his usual end of the sofa, then puts his legs up to lie back. I go to flop into the chair—I'd like something to happen, but all my planning skills have been used up for the day, so I figure I'll just sit in my usual seat until an opportunity comes up—but Paul says, "Sit here?" So then I go to sit up the other end, but he spreads his legs, and says, "Nah, here," patting the sofa between his legs. I do, and lean back against him, and he puts his arms around me. Strangely, it feels more intimate than anything we've done so far; but my brain is tired and slightly buzzed with beer, so I just enjoy the feeling rather than analysing it.

After a while his left hand starts roaming and makes its way under my shirt. He moves his hand in small sweeps at first, just across my belly, slightly ticklish; then the arcs become larger, reaching my pecs, brushing against them. It feels fantastic, and I wriggle back against him. Then with his right hand he undoes the button on my shorts, then the zip, and burrows in to grasp my cock, which is already mostly hard. It's the first time he's touched my cock with his hand, in spite of what we've already done. I was expecting something like his tradie handshake, but it's surprisingly light, his touch, up and down, up and circling the head with his thumb and forefinger, down and up and down. Then his left arm, across my sternum, tightens into that wrestler grip he likes, and I can feel him hard behind me, and he starts exhaling into the short hair at the back of my head, the short hair that's so sensitive on me. The sensation's suddenly gone from quiet to intense, and I go to say something, but then my body's gone rigid and I'm coming, partly over my belly and partly over his hand and partly inside my boxers.

"You're funny," he says.

"I'm funny, am I?"

"I don't mean you make me laugh—"

"I don't make you laugh?"

"That's not what I mean either. I just wasn't expecting it to be that intense for you, whatever it was that did it."

It's a real floaty high this time, the postejaculation bliss mixed with the buzz of the day, and I say, "It's just you." I realize belatedly that sounds too much like an admission of the scaring-away variety. But after that we still lie there: he doesn't seem scared off by my blundering confession; not yet anyway.

CHAPTER 7

I'M OUT of the house early on Sunday morning, buying cat stuff: a litter box, food bowls, toys, et cetera. Then I go and pick up the still-unnamed cat. She isn't happy to be in a cat carry cage in my rarely used car.

When I get back to the house, Paul is on the roof of his. He's wearing just shorts, a tool belt, and boots. I don't think my jaw actually drops, but inside my head I feel like one of those cartoon guys whose lower lip hits the pavement when he sees a cartoon girl, or perhaps Bugs Bunny dressed up as one.

"It's warm, eh." He grins, and then hooks one thumb into his belt and shorts, tugging them lower so the slope of his hipbone is visible.

"You—" I'm not sure what I want to say. I'd like it to be something clever, but there's no chance of that. There's a long pause.

"Yeah, me. I reckon that'd be the cat, then."

As he's climbing down the ladder, Sam comes out onto the front steps. "The cat!" I unlock my door and we go inside my house.

"That's it. She's your cat too, now. What do you want to call her?" I ask Sam. She's squatting down in front of the cage, looking through the mesh, saying hello. She pauses for a few seconds.

"Gabrielle." Gabi the tabby. Heh.

"I was just joking, y'know," says Paul in a quiet voice. "I don't really have tickets on myself." It's funny hearing him use this expression my gran would have used. I don't think he's arrogant; he's surprisingly lacking in arrogance, I think, given how good-looking he is. He still has drips of sweat rolling down him from working in the sun, even this early in the morning.

"I'm just going to the bathroom, then I'll set up everything. Back in a minute." As I go past him, I swipe a palm down his back and collect some of the sweat.

My jerking off takes about the minute I anticipated.

When I get back, Paul looks down at my crotch, which is still tented out. "Did you just—"

"Maybe."

He grins again.

I GO to bridge this week, straight from the office, since I'm working late again. I see a cat run out of a house just before I arrive, and think of Gabi. She's fitted in surprisingly quickly: the goth girl from the rescue society didn't know much about her history, but she'd obviously spent a lot of time inside a house, and needed only the minimal litter training I'd read up about. She's still a winner with Sam; Sam has managed to avoid being scratched, unlike me.

Lance comes to the door when I get there, kisses me. "Come in. We can start a second table now."

The same crew as last time are there, plus another regular and a new guy. Judging by the new guy's face he's now the youngest by far, maybe seven or eight years younger than me. Lance introduces us. "This is Gray, short for Graham. Gray, Aaron."

"Mr Fifty Shades," says James in a deliberately loud whisper to Oliver. Gray looks embarrassed. I shake his hand and hope James doesn't scare him off.

I grab some of the leftovers—Vietnamese summer rolls and dumplings—and seat myself. I'm partnering Lance, and Gray's to my left, Oliver to my right. While Lance is dealing, he asks, "So how's that young man of yours in LA? Any more photos?"

"He's not my young man anymore. Probably someone else's young man by now." Everyone else's young man, I'm tempted to say, just as a joke, but I'm sure it would be taken as bitterness even though I feel completely unmoved about it. I hadn't even thought of Xavier in a while.

"I'm so sorry," says Lance. "I blundered right in there."

"Don't worry. I'm not bothered about it. I think he was a bit too much of a partier for me anyway. You know, he didn't even play bridge."

"Didn't even play bridge!" exclaims Lance, and Oliver gasps in mock horror.

"So you can see I couldn't stay with him." Gray isn't saying anything, but I see him smiling out of the corner of my eye.

"What about that electrician neighbour of yours who reads the *Iliad*?"

"What about him?" I try not to sound like I'm hiding anything. Does Lance remember everything I tell him? I don't think I said anything beyond that. Then I realize it was before anything had happened, so there wouldn't have been anything to give away.

"Is he still reading interesting books?" That's obviously what caught Lance's attention as an editor.

"Just finished *An Open Swimmer*."

"Wonderful!" Then it's time to play.

The first game I get to gauge Gray's skills as declarer. He's not a complete novice and knows what he's doing, but doesn't play his cards especially confidently. Just generally shy, I guess. Oliver's being very encouraging, probably in part to make sure this twenty-something comes back as eye candy.

I'm dummy the second game, and as my mind is wandering— Lance is pretty certain to make the contract—I have an idea. I send Paul a text: *Beach on Saturday?* I expect he'll be asleep by now and not read the message until morning, but I get a response almost immediately.

For sure.

WE'RE READY to go early on Saturday, naturally. Paul's in board shorts and singlet, same as me, and Sam's just in her swimmers. Sam gets strapped into her car seat while I put a small esky with apples and water into the back of Paul's ute, followed by all the towels and sunscreen and other beach paraphernalia and a change of clothes for Sam.

"You want to drive?" asks Paul, handing me the keys.

"You sure?" I've never driven a ute before.

"Yeah. You know where we're going, and I still hate driving in these streets here."

"You drive them every day when you go to jobs."

"That's why I don't want to on the weekend too, eh."

"Fair enough."

The ute's a lot bigger than my car, so I'm exaggeratedly careful pulling out of the parking space and making sure I don't scrape nearby cars. Luckily, I don't smash anything, and we're on our way.

As we're driving, I say, "So you do have board shorts."

"Yeah," he says. "I can swim a bit. We'd go to the town pool sometimes, when it was really hot and I wasn't busy with farm work. It's just the ocean I haven't been to."

"How about Sam?"

"She's been to the pool a few times and loves the water, but can't go in over her head yet. It's just been the kiddie pool for her."

"Okay. She probably shouldn't go past waist-deep, then, for the first time. The waves can be a surprise—you don't realize how much force there is in them—and there are all the currents you don't get in a pool. You can't see them under the surface." I'm speaking to him too, but directing it at Sam makes it sound not too patronizing.

"Yeah, *An Open Swimmer* gave me an idea about how it'd be different."

The actual experience of it won't be something he can know in advance, I think.

When we get there, the beach isn't too busy: early morning surfers and keen swimmers, but not the hordes that will be here later in the day. While Paul and I are lumbered with supplies, Sam runs towards the ocean—the sand's not foot-burningly hot yet, fortunately. She stops before she gets to the waterline, uncertain about going in by herself, also fortunately.

Paul and I claim a spot on the sand and drop our stuff there. I shuck my singlet and board shorts.

"Is that what you wear swimming?" Paul asks, looking at my trunks. They're not even high-cut, more square.

"Yeah. Board shorts drag a lot in the water." I look down at them. "They're not much shorter than those shorts you wear."

"You wouldn't wear those back home."

"Good thing we're not at the ocean in inland Central Queensland, then."

"Fair enough."

"Want us to swing you?" I ask Sam as we walk towards her. "I used to do that with my little sister."

"Yeah!"

So we go down to the waterline and then just past, and take a hand each. The sand slopes away gently for the first part, and then drops more steeply farther out: I know it from previous visits. The waves are about knee height when they hit the shallows. We swing her, and on the count of three dunk her in one of the waves. She squeals and laughs, and squeals and laughs some more. "Again!" she says.

We decide it's enough after a dozen or so agains. "You want to go in first?" I ask Paul. One of us has to stop with Sam. "You want to build a sand castle?" I say to her.

"Yeah!"

As we choose a spot and settle in, I ask her about vacation care, which she just started yesterday, at Sveta's sister's place. "Who are the other kids there?"

"I don't know most of them yet. There's Finn. He's my friend. We played on the tyres."

That's a quick friendship. "Cool."

I look out from time to time to see where Paul is—he's just past waist-deep, one time trying to float on his back and another time coming up from diving under water—but mostly I focus on building with Sam. She's happy to have just a shapeless mound, but I make some walls for her and then a small splashing pool inside the walls as the front moat. Then she puts some seaweed in as a flag. She didn't want to touch it at first, so I threw it at her, and then she threw it back with an "eww," and then was willing to pick some up herself and decided that's exactly what the castle needed to be finished. It's funny how when she's pondering the seaweed placement, she has the exact same gesture Paul does, palm behind the head and elbow sticking up and out.

"I want Dad to see it."

"Okay, I'll go get him. You stay right here next to it so we can find it again."

She nods. "Okay."

I head out to where Paul is, half swimming and half wading. Just before I get to him I dunk my head—it's been too long since I've been completely immersed in the salty freshness. I should come to the beach more often.

When I get to Paul, he says, "So I haven't drowned yet."

"So I see." He starts walking towards me, using his arms to help propel himself along. When he's close he reaches out one hand and I pull him through the water towards me; and then, when he's really close, I feel his other hand down the back of my swimmers. "Christ," he says, "those togs, they're so tight, it's like you're not wearing anything."

I laugh. "Come on, you've got a castle to inspect." But I don't pull away as his hand keeps exploring into the cleft. I wonder if he'd like to fuck me, or whether that's a long time away yet. Wonder if me fucking him is a longer time away still. I reach behind me: he's hard, in spite of the morning coolness of the water, and I grab on. "Come on."

At waist-deep, there's finally a large wave. I dive under, but Paul elects to crash face-first into it and goes under. He surfaces, shaking his head. "They're stronger than you think, those waves."

ON THE way home we pick up burgers for dinner and eat them in the car. Sam's asleep before we get back, and Paul carries her inside to bed. I follow with the rest of the stuff.

"You want to have a shower here?" he asks. Sam had washed off at the beach at one of those outdoor showers and then Paul had got her changed, but Paul and I had just stayed in swimmers, beach towels around our waists for the ute trip back.

"Heh, yeah."

"Okay, I'll have a quick one first."

I'm going to suggest having one together, but he's gone before I can say anything. I stand around—I don't want to sit on anything in a damp beach towel—but not for long: he is indeed quick. He's just wearing a blue bath towel wrapped around his waist, much shorter than the beach one was. He's really sexy like that.

When I go into the bathroom, I realize it wouldn't have been practical to shower together anyway. I haven't used this bathroom before. While, as with everything else, the shape is basically a mirror of my own house's, a previous renovation has made it very different. And it's a renovation that seems to have been done fairly poorly, with tiles skewed and cracked, concrete showing signs of decay. I imagine this is one of the areas of the house Paul is fixing up. There's a tiny shower next to the bath, barely big enough for one adult. I'm about to step in, and realize I don't have a towel; open the door to call out to Paul and discover one placed on the floor.

After I finish the shower, I go into his room—that's where I'm guessing he'll be—and I'm right, as he grabs me from behind the door. His hands are on my shoulders and he propels me towards the bed. A light pressure on the top of my shoulders tells me he wants me to sit on the bed, so I do.

Then, surprising me, he unwraps my towel and kneels between my legs. He looks up at me, down at my cock, up again, then down. My cock's started stirring more—it was already stirring from the shower invitation—and then, lifting it up with one hand, he takes it soft into his mouth. Mostly soft, although that's changing pretty quickly. He takes it out, and when he goes for it again, it's erect. This is more difficult, and after just putting his lips over the head—mirroring what I did to him that other evening, I think—he tries to go deeper.

I wince. "Gotta watch teeth." He pulls off, and then tries again, covering his teeth with his lips. That's better—so much better—although I'm not sure how long he'll be able to keep it up for. My first time I didn't manage it for long before my mouth got tired. So I focus on looking at him, his broad back, his arms braced on my legs, tufts of his armpit hair just visible; then I run my hands up and down through the short hair on the back of his head. I hadn't anticipated how much this would speed things up, so I only manage an "I'm, uh—" and pull his head off before coming on his chin and his neck. He looks at my wet cock, slick with both spit and semen, and then up at me, and smiles. He touches the come on his neck and examines his fingers.

"It wasn't like I expected. I thought it would taste—stronger. But it just tasted like you, and maybe sort of like the ocean, too, a bit, even after the shower. Anyway, I know I'm not any good at it yet."

"That was awesome. And it's not like there's anyone rating performance. 'That was a 3.5 degree of difficulty blow job, Leon, and he's pulled it off.' Heh."

Paul laughs. "So can I come on you now?"

"Anytime." He's looking at my chest, and it doesn't take him long to splatter all over it.

After, as he's lying next to me, he says, "I was thinking about two things."

"Yeah?"

"What do you reckon about a gate between our backyards? Sam's pretty taken with the cat, so I thought that that way she could come and see her without going on to the street and forgetting to close the front door." He turns his face to me on the pillow and looks at me tentatively.

"Sounds like a great idea. Let me know what I can do."

"Cut the gate out with a jigsaw?"

"Err, no, I don't have one."

"Drill the hinges?"

"No, no drill either. Stop teasing me." He's laughing. "I can hold the gate while you're drilling, I guess. Anyway, what was the second thing?"

"You probably already have plans, but—Sam and I are going to my parents' property for Christmas, staying for a couple of weeks. I've had friends come and visit before, my parents don't mind at all; like it, really. It'll be hilarious for them having a city slicker friend of mine come and stay."

Okay, I get the friend message, but I do understand. And notwithstanding that plea—make sure my parents don't see anything weird, anything beyond friendship—I'm touched that he's asked me.

"When are you going?"

"Two days before Christmas."

I calculate. "I'll be having Christmas with my parents and Deelie. But maybe I could come Boxing Day, if that's okay." I can go down to Melbourne earlier, take a few days off, so I can spend as much time as I'd planned to with Deelie, just brought forward a bit. I'll check whether Howie can look after Gabi, or failing that book someone through the vet to come and look in on her and refill her food and water.

He gives me a quick kiss. Kisses usually happen while we're having sex, or before, not afterwards. I smile at him and put my head on his chest.

THE FOLLOWING Friday evening is when I meet Paul's ex-wife Kaylee. Not meet, exactly. From my desk I hear some arguing in the street, sounding heated, and I hope it's not a repeat of the disagreement between two drunken pub-goers from a few months ago that led to another neighbour's car window being smashed.

So I go out my front door, and it's Paul and a woman. Paul is facing away from me and doesn't see me, but the woman scowls at me, so I put up my hands in a sorry-to-intrude-on-you way and go back inside. I sit at my desk again, and even though the window's open because it's been such a warm day—I don't shut it, even though that would be polite—I don't hear anything they're saying, just the hisses and growls of bad feeling. It could be a disgruntled customer of Paul's whose wiring is still faulty, I think, but that's rather unlikely.

Almost certainly Kaylee. I think she was pretty, although the scowl made it hard to tell.

I do see Paul carrying a sleeping Sam out to a car, and then Kaylee taking off with more of a screech of tyres than is strictly necessary.

Shortly after that Paul comes to my door.

"That was Kaylee." The anger's still there.

"Uh-huh."

"She just came to get Sam—change of plan. She was supposed to pick her up tomorrow, but she's just decided, just right now, that she's leaving early in the morning, going somewhere with this new guy of hers, so it was more convenient for her to pick up Sam now, even though she's already asleep." The word "convenient" is layered with scorn.

"Want a beer?" I ask.

"I dunno what I want. Yeah, a beer, ta."

When I come back with one, he takes it and puts it down on the table, and then grabs the bottom of my T-shirt and starts pulling it over my head. The beer will have to wait.

THE NEXT day we go to the beach again—I suggest it hoping that it will banish Paul's lingering annoyance with Kaylee, and it appears to do the job almost instantaneously. As he goes next door to gather his stuff—he stayed the night for the first time last night, and until then I'd forgotten how much I missed it, that half waking at random times and feeling an arm across my belly or a chest to my back—he asks, "I don't s'pose you have another pair of those togs, do you?"

As it happens, I do have another pair, one other pair. I don't comment as I go and get them from my chest of drawers and throw them to him.

"Ta."

We don't get there quite as early as last time, but there's still enough space. And then it's a day for going with whatever whim takes hold. Swim. Doze. Read: continuing with the ocean theme, we're both reading Witi Ihimaera's *Whale Rider*; I finish that while Paul's still going on it, and move on to Ihimaera's *Nights in the Gardens of Spain*, his gay novel. Get sandwiches from the kiosk. Swim some more, to cool our sun-stretched skin. Paul's still wearing his board shorts until this post-lunch swim, then he strips them off—I can detect the self-consciousness—and he's wearing my swimmers underneath, which are a bit tighter on him than they are on me. There are a couple of teenage girls on nearby towels, maybe early twenties, who have been watching us, and I think from their furious whispering have been debating whether to come over or at least wander past to check Paul out: as Paul's dropping his boardies, they take a photo of him, and another as he's stretching. I smile. He's pretty clueless. I wonder if those photos will end up across the Internet. I get my own phone out, beckon him. "Hey." He looks over then turns to me, puts his hands on his hips, dragging the swimmers down slightly as he does so that his hipbones show, as he did that shirtless time on the roof; and grins. I take the photo.

Later in the day, there's a different woman with a friend who asks Paul if he could take a photo of her and her friend: she leans forward for the photo, close to falling out of her bikini top. When she goes to take her phone back, thanking Paul effusively, I hear her say something about putting his number in her phone. I keep reading.

"Collecting admirers?" I ask when he's lying on his towel again.

"Nah. Mentioned having a five-year-old, that scared her off. Wasn't my type anyway." He smiles and touches my elbow with his own.

The sun's low in the sky when we leave. Back home I follow Paul into his house. He takes first shower again. When it's my turn, I take out of my board shorts pocket what I'd prepared this morning, just in case the signs seemed propitious, and they do judging by Paul's towel-wrapped body as he left the bathroom. I put the condom to one side, and then after my shower use the two packets of lube on myself, one finger inside and then two. This might be overly cautious, getting myself ready in here—just in case he might be put off by the warm-up before he tries the main event—but I always like to be prepared.

When I go to his room, he's sprawled on the bed, towel still on him. He goes to get up, but I say, "My turn to suggest something," and throw the condom to him. "What do you think?"

"Really?" He looks hesitant. "I'd do you?"

"Yeah. If you want. I mean, that's what I want. Like, really really want."

Looking at him on the bed is having its usual effect, and my cock's rising. I still have some lube on my left hand, so I pull his towel apart with my right and rub it on the head of his cock: he shivers. Then I straddle him so that his cock is between the cheeks of my arse and slide along, forward and back, once. He bucks his hips and I know that he's up for it.

As he's opening the condom packet, I'm kissing along the inside of his thighs, and it's not long before he's at the right hardness. "It's been a while for me," I say, "so you'll probably have to go slower than you'd be used to." With a woman, I don't say. "It's easier if we go like this." I'm straddling him again while he's lying on the bed, and I lower myself onto him. I can feel the head, wanting entrance. "This time." And then I don't talk any more. It's good that I prepped myself in the bathroom, but still, I forget what it's like after such a long stretch without it. I clench my teeth. Lower, lower. Breathe. Good thing I have strong leg muscles from cycling, to keep from just collapsing down. Lower. Paul's patient, but I feel the tremors in his hips. Then he's all in. My hands are on his shoulders. I pause, head hanging, then look up at his face. He really is beautiful, blue eyes and blond scruff and strong jaw. Then I start the rhythm and he joins it, and my prostate and my heart both spark at the same time.

IT'S ABOUT an hour later, and we're lying there, my front to his back.

"Okay if I stay?" I ask. "Sam won't be back early, will she?"

"Yeah, nah, stay." Then he rolls over, and rolls me over too, so his front is now to my back. "Could we, maybe, do that again?"

I laugh. "I didn't know if you'd like it."

"How could I not like it? It was—mate." That last word stretches out. He wraps me in his wrestler hold and starts grinding.

"Do you have another condom?" I ask. "I only brought one. Didn't want to presume too much."

"Ah, no."

"Really?"

"Yeah, really. I didn't expect—with Sam and all, I didn't think I'd have time for anything. Not until later, when I'd settled in and sorted things out. Didn't want anything anyway. I didn't expect you."

I didn't expect you either. "I can't really duck back next door to get another one like this. Maybe that backyard gate will come in handy when we make it."

"Yeah, when we make it." He laughs, and his grinding speeds up. "I guess I'll have to make do with this instead." And he does.

CHAPTER 8

ONE OF the afternoons I'm home early, Sam comes through the back gate that Paul and I made on Sunday. It was mostly Paul, of course, it worked out as I'd expected with me just holding things. The gate's really just kid height, stopping halfway up the fence, but I can get through if I crouch. She goes back through it and then into my yard again, for the novelty of it. Gabi sticks her nose out the back door and sees that there's something she hasn't investigated yet, so she bounds outside and then jumps through the gate too.

After a while, Paul looks over the fence. "Seems to be working okay, the new gate."

"Yep. Actually, I have a favour to ask that requires your skills too. The downlights in my kitchen aren't working, not just the globes but something else, some wiring thing, and it'll be hard to cook without them. And I mean, not a freebie—I'll pay—it's a favour because I know you've knocked off work already."

"Don't be stupid, you won't pay. Let me just get my tools."

While I'm waiting, Gabi goes back inside, followed by Sam. And then Paul clambers through the gate, wearing his tool belt but no shirt, as he had on the roof.

"Warm," we say together, and I roll my eyes.

"Jeez you're a tease," I say quietly.

"Dunno what you mean." Then he strokes the head of his screwdriver, grips the tool lightly with his hand, slides it up and down once, then twice. "Okay, where are these problem lights?"

He takes out a globe and puts in a new one—to see whether I'd actually checked properly, I suppose, which feels vaguely insulting except that I'm sure he's had lots of customers who also claimed they'd checked the globe and who'd somehow not—and when he sees that it's still not working, takes out two more and starts inspecting the wiring.

While he's laying out some of his tools, I check to see whether Sam's around and, with the coast clear, give him a quick kiss on the neck. He reaches behind to give me a grope in return. "I don't reckon I need you to hold anything for me this time. You know, just in case you have to go to the bathroom."

THE WORK Xmas event is at a nice location, with a balcony right out on the water. The event's been going for a little while when I arrive. I find Dean; he's wearing an unflattering striped shirt.

"Are you going out clubbing after this?" he asks me.

I'm not that dressed up. "No, not planning to."

I look around the room. Out of about forty software engineers in the office here, there are seven women. The best-looking one unwisely didn't bring her boyfriend this year, and is being chatted up by a member of another team who's well on the way to being drunk. I can hear him from where we're standing: "So how would you feel about doing some pair programming with me sometime?" I don't hear her response, but I do see her face. There's another engineer talking to his project manager, anger on his face, a stiffly pointed finger poking the air from the hand not holding a glass. Just like a typical work Xmas party, really. If it had been at the office, there would have been someone photocopying their buttocks.

I check out the rest of the attendees and look to see which ones might be gay, just for statistical purposes. None of the software engineers are, to my knowledge. That's a bit unusual—there were a few at uni. There are a couple of guys in accounts or sales, an area I don't have much to do with; one's here, and has brought his boyfriend again this year. There does seem to be a new guy who—I catch him looking at me. I smile at him. He looks away, then looks back and smiles. Heh. Two out of forty now, I reckon.

Some other software engineers drift in our direction. I'd made a bet with myself that talk would fairly quickly turn to the upcoming Star Wars movie, and it only takes about ten minutes before it does. It's fun, though. There's some pontificating about the Expanded

90

Universe and then about JJ Abrams, whether he's a genius or totally unsuitable, which I don't really join in as I don't have an opinion. I do, after a few drinks, join in with a mock lightsaber battle with Chris, who's back in Sydney, for some reason I'm not clearly understanding. I do notice New Guy looking over again while I'm being dorky. Oh well. Good thing I'm not looking for someone.

THE BRIDGE Xmas event is just like the regular sessions, but with about half as much bridge playing and three times as much food and wine. I bring a Spanish potato tortilla I made last night—essentially a quiche, the Anglo-Saxon world's gayest food, and so perfectly suited.

"Wonderful, quiche," says Lance, smiling, when I arrive and hand it to him. He's in with the joke too.

There are about twenty people there, some of whom I haven't seen for a long time. Oliver is on the way to drunk already—he's a happy drunk, essentially just louder than usual—and he comes to drape himself over me. I give him a kiss on the cheek; he goes to turn his lips to me, but his reflexes are slowed. He's happy to make a joke of it. "Curses, almost got some tongue in."

Gray's there too. He has an audience, all guys who weren't here when he first came along. It doesn't seem exactly like a conversation, more like they're pitching questions to him and he's answering them but not managing to turn it into more than an information exchange; he looks nervous. I wave over to him and after I've talked a bit more to Oliver—he's joined my gym, and does some spot-on impersonations of some of the other gym-goers I know, making me laugh—I find Gray standing next to me. He hangs around, mostly silent at first, but eventually Oliver and I get him to be part of our conversation, which has moved on to movies and theatre by that stage.

Later I'm talking to Lance. "I think Gray might be the teensiest bit keen on you," he says.

"He was probably just hanging around because I'm about his age." Relative to everyone else here, that's broadly true.

"He seems nice."

"Stop matchmaking. I'm not really wanting to get into anything at the moment. So if you're right—I'm not saying you are, mind—I'll make sure to be careful."

THE LAST in the series of Xmas events is drinks with uni friends, Howie and Sveta and whoever else wants to come. Paul wants to come. He's wearing his going-out clothes, the blue shirt with the cuffs folded back and the blue jeans, already there with Sveta when I arrive at the pub from work. They're talking about her sister's day care, and how Sam's getting along, when I ask if they want another drink.

When I get back Howie's arrived too—this is early for him—and I slip in between him and Paul. "Too slow. You'll have to get your own drink." Others arrive too: Vijay who I last saw playing footie in the park, John of the day-care sagas, Joe who I haven't seen for a long time, now in legal advice for charitable bequests or something.

When Howie comes back, I turn away slightly from the others, towards him. It's time for a chat, I think, some dispensing of advice by me. I can feel Paul's leg with my own, touching as if by accident; he doesn't move away.

"Cheers," I say to Howie.

"Cheers."

"So, that Mandy from the party. You seeing her? You seemed pretty keen. Plus I haven't been hearing about your terrible relationship drought."

He laughs. "I was, but she's gone back to Ireland now. We knew it would just be a short-time thing, but it was pretty great. She was pretty great. It was like…." He trails off, doesn't finish his thought.

"It was like it used to be when you'd be going out with the sort of girls you'd hang out with at uni or house parties?"

"Yeah." He looks reflective.

"You know, they're really the only girls I've seen who make you light up like that. Not like the one-off dates with models or whatever." I hear a lot about the modelling events, the parties, and the after-parties, and the after-after-parties—they're partly fun, partly career moves—and they seem to take a lot of his attention: the women from there are what he sees all the time, and also, with their glamour and attractiveness, what he'd focus on, understandably. Constant sugar-rushes seeing one hot woman after another: eye candy. Probably something you'd only notice if you have a chance to step back and think about it.

"Yeah." Still pondering; then his head flicks up to meet my gaze, and he smiles. "You're a relationship genius! Which isn't something I'd expect to say to someone who'd had their own eighteen-month drought. You met anyone since that Xavier from LA?"

"No." I'd rather not lie to Howie, but even if I hadn't promised Paul, I wouldn't say anything before checking with him. I still don't know how he actually thinks of this anyway. Of us. "Maybe we can figure out what I want next time."

"I'll drink to that."

At the lull in our own conversation, I hear Sveta and Paul and Joe.

"—the clients love it if you can talk about literature," Joe is saying, "the great books and whatnot." He turns to Paul. "Maybe it doesn't matter not to know about all of that in your line of work, I suppose." I want to wipe that smarmy expression, that pretend friendliness, off his face. Paul's expression is neutral.

"Hey, books," I interject. "Paul and I are in this book club, we're reading Ihimaera at the moment."

"Imaira?" Joe stumbles over the name.

"*Whale Rider*!" says Sveta. "That was great. Ihimaera's really one of New Zealand's best writers. Super book, super movie." I don't know if she's actually read the book or seen the movie, but when we exchange glances, I see she wants to put Joe in his place too.

"Yeah. We've finished that one already, now we're on to *Nights in the Garden of Spain*." As I'm saying it, I'm not sure I should mention the gay novel, but I can't off the top of my head think of the names of his other novels. Probably no one knows it anyway.

"I've heard that's good," she says, on cue. Then, pointedly turning her shoulder towards Joe, she says to me, "Now that you've finished talking to Howie, I was going to ask you if you could help out with this thing Katarina is organizing and that Sam will be going to." As Joe takes the hint and moves to talk to someone else who's arrived more recently, she says, "*Mudak*." I nod and repeat it.

Paul still has a neutral expression on his face.

Sveta lowers her voice, talking to Paul. "I don't know why we still hang out with him. So full of himself. He barely scrapped through"—I guess she means "scraped" here—"but now he talks as if he has all civilization's wisdom in himself." She's quiet enough, but it's possible Joe can still hear. It's possible she doesn't care.

"Yeah, he name-drops the uni all the time, for some imagined status," I say. "Really overcompensating."

Paul shrugs. "Well, a sparky doesn't need to go to uni." I want to smack Joe across the head. Paul takes another sip. "What does *mudak* mean anyway?"

"Prick," I say.

"Or asshole," says Sveta. "Very useful word."

This turns out to be only a minor blip during the evening; after that Paul just sticks with Howie and Sveta and me, and Ted when he shows up later, and the rest of the evening is fun.

MY FIRST full day in Melbourne, staying with Deelie at our parents' house—although neither of them are back from overseas yet—we go to the National Gallery of Victoria. One of the exhibitions is a slightly psychedelic look at the Congo and its violence, men with guns in the midst of vegetation that's oddly coloured, thanks to some photographic distortion; it makes me want to go and read *Heart of Darkness*. Also somewhat psychedelic is a virtual reality display that presents an artist's imagining of a dystopian future, filled with endless geometric patterning and naked pink figures merging into each other: I'm feeling queasy by the end of it. To recover, we go and check out Rupert Bunny in the regular collections. I like his paintings—when I hear myself say that, it has echoes of "I may not know much about art, but I know what I like"—Deelie by now knows more art history than I do, and has definite tastes, but she likes his paintings too. Some of Bunny's work is just typical late-nineteenth-century pictures of the bourgeoisie in gardens—think *Déjeuner sur l'herbe*, with the clothed men and naked women having a picnic, but less famous—but others are striking, *Sea Idyll* with the curve to the main figure's smooth back echoing the curve of the wave, or *Out of the Sea*, with some weird Lovecraftian sea monster in the centre and a fleeing human in the foreground; still a connection to our earlier psychedelic experiences.

Over a milkshake, I get an update of what Deelie's thinking about career-wise. Currently she's tossing up between the artistic option of photographer or the practical option of working at the Department of Foreign Affairs and Trade via a law degree. Our mother's a partner in a multinational legal consulting firm, and Deelie doesn't want to do that, doesn't want her life consumed by a job that way, but she does like the international aspect of it, the opportunity to go to places like France that the both of us came to love growing up.

The next day I go with her to paintball. She and her art friends had organized it, and I'd said I'd come along once I knew I'd be here for it. We get all suited up in the camouflage gear, although I don't put the jacket on yet because it's warm, just stay in my singlet; before we go through the training, some of Deelie's friends are giggling, and ask her something.

She comes over, rolls her eyes. "Some of them want a photo with you at the start. I can't imagine why."

Probably just because it's an all-girl school they go to. "Sure."

"I mean, I've told them you're a dork, and a gay dork at that, but they still want the photo."

I walk over to them and two of them, giggling some more, give Deelie their cameras. "Practice for a photographic future," I say. She rolls her eyes again.

After that we go through the training and the warnings about face masks, goggles, neck and throat protection, dangerous shots, dangerous behaviour. Even as I'm walking out onto the ground, I'm not sure how I'll bring myself to shoot teenage girls. Then I think about

Mean Girls—that'll help me see them as vicious threats. I manage to shoot one crouching in a wooden fort, and then another inexpertly hidden behind a tree, but then I'm hit. Deelie survives until the end.

As I drive us home in a rental car, I look over at her. She has a bruise forming on her right arm. I don't know what from. "Heh, warrior princess."

"You don't still watch that, do you?"

"Maybe. There's a kid next door up in Sydney and I've watched some episodes with her."

I can't talk about Paul with anyone, although sometimes it wants to bubble up out of me; this is the next best thing. Just touching on it, skirting the edges of it without actually giving anything away.

"Oh my God."

"She's pretty fierce, this kid."

Last week on a visit through the back gate, Sam told me what she'd been up to at vacation care. As well as doing craft and going on an excursion to the park, she updated me on her playground relationships.

"Finn's my frenemy," she told me.

I wasn't even aware that five-year-olds knew the word "frenemy."

"Do you know what a frenemy is?"

"Someone who's kind of a friend and kind of an enemy."

So apparently they do know.

"Why are you frenemies?" I asked.

"We were playing Xena, and he was a baddie, and when I kicked him by accident, he hit me back on purpose."

"Did you say sorry?"

"It was an accident."

"You should still say sorry, though. Xena would if it was an accident." That's probably not in the canon, but I'm happy to make this up.

"Okay."

I tell Deelie a bit more about Sam as I'm driving.

OUR PARENTS have arrived back by Christmas Day. They've been cooking together in the kitchen in the morning—roast duck, a cassoulet-like side dish, parsnips and green beans, a tiramisu for dessert—and we've just set the table and sat down to eat.

"Did we tell you that your father and I managed to meet up in New York and see *Hamilton*?" They were both travelling separately for work, but in recent years they'd tried to arrange things so that they could still join up. When I was finishing school and Deelie was still small, they'd been away but always apart, building their careers. I've wondered if they made a deliberate decision to try to be together more, whether they'd drifted apart but come to a realization that they wanted to stay together. Now they do things together—like cooking the lunch today—that keep them in touch. They still have to travel a lot, my mother with her legal work and my father with finance, so the time they've found to spend together doesn't usually extend to Deelie and me. So perhaps our relationship isn't as close as other friends have with their parents, but I still think they're pretty good as people go, our parents.

"No, nothing about *Hamilton*. How was it?" I ask. "One of my friends has the cast recording already and is raving about it."

"Impressive," says my mother. "I'm not one for rap"—neither am I—"but the lyrics were outstanding. The whole show too. Apparently they had the historian who wrote Hamilton's biography as consultant. After seeing the show, I want to read that now."

"How's the duck?" asks my father.

"It's great." Still a bit pink in the middle, as it should be.

"Now, I know we don't really do Christmas presents anymore." Deelie and I do with each other: this year I got her a DSLR camera, and she got me the shirt I'm wearing for lunch. "But we thought that with Cordelia's sixteenth birthday coming up in a few months, and the driver's license that comes with that, we thought we'd combine them together. So maybe we could go and look at cars next week. Just a small one as a starter."

"Thanks, Mum, Dad." Deelie looks pleased.

"You're off again tomorrow, right, Aaron?" asks my father. "Work?"

"Not this time. A friend's invited me to his parents' property in Queensland."

"A friend? Are you seeing anyone at the moment?" My mother's dark eyes, so like mine—Deelie and I both take after her, dark hair and dark eyes, slender build, although her hair is greying now—her eyes focus on me.

"No, it's just a friend. I was seeing someone in LA, but it didn't work with the distance." She and my father share a look.

"Xavier," says Deelie. "Do you still see him when you go back?"

"Yes. There's no bad feelings."

CHAPTER 9

THE PROPERTY isn't easy to get to. I fly to Emerald via Brisbane; at the Emerald airport luggage carousel, I look around to see if Paul's there, since he told me I'd be picked up. Instead of him I see a couple, in their fifties probably: the woman's quite short, with sun-bleached hair and a tan; the man's wearing an Akubra and has his arms crossed above a beer gut, but taking those away, and the extra wrinkles, he looks a lot like Paul. I'm guessing they're his parents.

"Hi, I'm Aaron." I shake both their hands. Perhaps handshakes are partly genetic, judging by Paul's father. I hope mine was sufficiently firm.

"Hi, Aaron. I'm Barb, and this is Jack," says Paul's mother. "Fatty wanted to come, but we had some things to do in town—I had to drop off some clothes, and Jack had to see the vet about coming to look at some cattle—so we told him not to worry, we'd find you."

Pretty much all the other passengers on the small Brisbane-to-Emerald plane looked like locals, so I'm sure I stood out like a sore thumb. "It's good of you to come and get me. Thanks."

"Don't mention it. Any more bags?"

Maybe they think I need to bring a massive wardrobe with me, coming from the city. "No, this is it, didn't bring much. I hope it's not black tie for dinner."

Jack laughs. "No chance."

We walk out to their ute, in the car park. It's a dual cab one, with a giant roo bar on the front, and there's a kid seat in the back; I hop in next to that, sitting in the middle of the backseat. Jack drives.

"Have you been out in the country here before?" Barb asks.

"Not here. I've driven around in New South Wales—Dubbo and Bathurst and Orange—and rural Victoria, but nowhere around here."

"Very different here," says Jack. I believe it. "Fatty said that you do something with computers?"

"That's right. I've just been working with some Americans so they can get all the data they need about environmental hazards on their computers."

"Data, eh? I've got this computer at home that I'm having trouble connecting to the Internet. Do you reckon you could help?"

"Jack," says Barb, "he's just arrived for a holiday. He doesn't want to be looking at your computer."

"Sure, I don't mind. I do appreciate you having me come up here."

"Our pleasure. We like it when our children's friends stay. Make sure you tell us if there's anything you don't like. You're not a vegetarian, are you?"

"Not at all. I'll be happy with whatever." There isn't really anything I don't like, and if there were, there's no way I'd be a princess about it. "By the way, why do you call him Fatty? After Fatty Vautin?"

Jack laughs. "Yeah. Barb's brother was a huge fan when Vautin was still playing, and he started calling Paul that when he was small."

I gaze at the landscape outside the ute as we're driving along. It's still a fairly major road, even though we're out of Emerald now. "It looks pretty dry at the moment. Has the El Niño hit yet?" I've done some research before coming.

Jack sucks in air between his teeth. "We knew it was coming, so we've sold down a lot of our cattle. It's just starting to take hold—"

"The roos are at plague levels," says Barb. "The grass is all dry, and they're all over the place, eating it, so there won't be much feed coming up."

They fill me in on the weather for the rest of the trip. I relax: I've got them chatting comfortably. First hurdle passed.

A while after we've turned off onto a dirt road, the kangaroos become more frequent, and Barb's description of plague proportions isn't looking like an exaggeration. The ute's slowed to twenty kilometres an hour so that we don't hit one, which notwithstanding the roo bar would be unpleasant, I'm sure.

Finally we arrive at the house. It's quite large, a traditional Queenslander, with a veranda that goes all the way around. There are a few sheds that I can see, and another older ute; there's bound to be more that I can't see, since I know it's a large property. When we go inside, before my eyes adjust from the bright sun, I hear a "Hi, Aaron." It's Sam.

"Hi, Sam."

"Have you seen my remote control car yet?"

"No," says a male voice. "He's only just arrived, so he hasn't seen anything yet." It's Paul. Fatty. I go and shake his hand. It's funny how strongly the absence of only a few days makes me want to do more than shake his hand, much more, yank him in towards me and … but I know the deal. It stays a manly shake, nothing beyond that.

"I thought Aaron could stay in Dale's old room," says Barb. I know Dale is Paul's older brother.

"Whatever fits in with you." I follow her to a medium-sized room with a single bed. There are still some remnants of Dale's teenage years, a rugby league poster, another poster with Hunters and Collectors. I think of their music: "Throw Your Arms Around Me." Heh.

I stay long enough to deposit my bag and take out the presents I'd bought, and then head back to the living room.

The first one's for Jack and Barb: whiskey and chocolate. "That's to say thanks for having me here."

Barb opens it. "Thanks," she says. "You really didn't need to. But I do like a whiskey and soda."

"I don't know that one," says Jack. It's Laphroaig.

"It's just one I like, kind of smoky." While I'm talking, I'm watching Sam. She's looking at me expectantly. "Do you think there might be something for you?"

"Yes?"

"And you're right. Merry Christmas for yesterday."

She shakes the box I hand her. "Is it Lego?"

"Open it. But yes, it's Lego." It's one that has some flying horses and an air chariot in it.

She's ripped off the paper. "Is that Xena?" She points to one of the figurines on the box.

It's a non-copyright-infringing clone of Xena. "Yep."

"Awesome!"

"What do you say?" Paul reminds her.

"Thank you."

"And just so you don't feel left out, there's something for you," I say to him. I hand him an envelope.

"You shouldn't have." He looks like I shouldn't have. I should have gotten my excuse straight out there.

"Hey, it's not a Christmas present. It's for inviting me here, and—" I turn to his parents. "—he did some electrical work for me for free, and I wanted to say thanks. I wouldn't feel right taking advantage of nice neighbours."

Paul holds up the two football tickets I got him, for a game in the middle of next year. Tickets are already selling out for those. I think he looks pleased. "State of Origin tickets," he says to his parents. "Thanks."

"Would you like a beer?" asks Jack.

The answer has to be yes. "I would, thanks."

WE'RE ON our third beer—Paul and his dad and I are sitting on the veranda at the back of the house, and Sam's riding around on a very old trike that she's almost too big for—and we're talking politics. It's actually surprisingly not problematic. In one of my imagined scenarios, Paul's parents and I disagree about everything and I force myself to stay silent for my whole visit.

"The two big supermarket chains abuse their duopoly position," Jack is saying as if he's expecting disagreement.

"They're getting a pretty bad reputation, at least with people I talk to about it," I respond. "They really screw farmers, just for profit, even though they pretend they're doing it for the consumer's good. That whole milk thing they do, helping families or whatever their slogan is. I've read about their negotiating tactics with suppliers, real David and Goliath stuff; my friends and I all buy farmers' co-op milk now."

Paul's dad appears to be an old-style agrarian socialist: he's in total agreement. "We sell some beef to them, can't get away from that, but we've started diversifying with some specialist buyers. Even south of Queensland."

"Yeah, they're getting popular. Where we live has quite a few places that care about where their meat comes from, so there'd be scope there." I look at Paul, who's been quiet; just happy to listen, I think. "Sorry. I get carried away talking about politics."

"Or books." He smiles.

"Paul was a one for books when he was younger, not that we had many. We thought that of all of the kids, he might have stayed at school longer, but he just wanted to get out and do something practical."

Barb brings out another beer for each of us; she joins us, and we open the beers. I hope I don't have a hangover tomorrow.

"Thanks, love," says Jack. "Back on supermarkets, maybe Clive Palmer can shake things up."

Sigh. I couldn't expect agreement all the way through this drinking session. Clive Palmer: our version of Donald Trump or Silvio Berlusconi. Smaller in scale—not physically, where he's much larger in scale—only a federal Member of Parliament from Queensland, but with all the ridiculous ideas and dodgy wealth that they have. What to do? Let it pass and implicitly agree? Couldn't hurt. But on beer number four, my mouth and my brain aren't totally in sync.

"Can't agree about Clive. He's in so much trouble with his Chinese deals, he won't have any time to do anything useful, I reckon...." That's more polite than what I actually think.

The disagreement that follows, though, is as enjoyable as the earlier conversation has been. As Jack sloshes some of his beer around while waving his hand to make a point, Paul smiles at me. I smile back before returning to the argument.

THE NEXT day I don't have a hangover, fortunately, so I'm ready for a proposed early morning tour of the property. We won't actually be seeing all of it, or even much of it—we'll be going out on a quad bike, and it's more for the fun that Sam has in riding in the trailer. We'll just be going for a short low-speed ride around in essentially a big circle.

It's a relatively new-looking bike, and it has a passenger trailer that hooks onto the tow bar. Sam's excited—it could well be her favourite thing about visiting her grandparents—and she's watching closely as it's connected up. Jack's up and about as well, and helps strap Sam in with the makeshift seatbelt. He tells me I should wear a pair of the old Blundstone boots that they have lying around, like the ones that Paul wears when he's doing work on his house, rather than my newish sneakers. When I arrived I saw them all lined up, about half a dozen pairs with worn elastic sides, obviously just for slipping on if you need to go out on the property. So I find a pair that fits and swap, and now I'm set.

I sit behind Paul on the bike. He starts it up and engages the throttle, picking up a little speed until we're doing about fifteen kilometres an hour according to the speedo, although it feels faster not being enclosed like a car. Sam's yelling out behind me, some wordless release of excitement.

The ground's fairly flat, and there aren't a lot of trees around, mostly isolated stands of eucalyptus in this part of the property. There are some cattle in the middle distance, past a fence, I guess in a separate paddock. They're near a watering hole with a few more trees growing up around it, keeping to the shade and drinking occasionally.

As I'm looking around, I feel Paul scooch back, arms out almost at full stretch to hold on to the handlebars, so he's right up against me.

"Faster, faster," chants Sam.

"No way," Paul calls over his shoulder.

I take that moment to wrap my arms around Paul. "It's too fast for me already. I think I'm going to fall off!"

I can hear Sam laugh.

WHEN WE get back, my legs in particular are all sweaty. I'd brought jean shorts, as something that was casual and sturdy, but hadn't realized how different the heat would be here: the heavy material really traps the heat next to my skin. At home, I'd just take them off and walk around in my underwear, but that's not an option here.

Paul comes to the rescue as he sees me pulling them away from my legs to cool down. "Do you want to borrow some footie shorts? They're pretty much a uniform around here."

That's actually a good idea. "Yeah, thanks."

He goes into his room to find a pair and then tosses them to me. I go into my room to change—well, first to sniff the shorts to see if they have any of Paul's scent, but disappointingly they just smell like laundry detergent—and find I'm probably an inch smaller around the waist than Paul, so I have to pull the drawstring about as tight as it will go, although my leg muscles—and gluteal muscles too, I guess—help keep them up.

I go out and put on the pair of old boots I was wearing for the quad bike ride, and find Paul on the veranda by himself. I lean against one of the veranda pillars, thumbs in the still-loose waistband of the shorts. "Could I be a convincing tradie? 'Hi, you called about needing something serviced? Let me show you my toolbox.'" I leer.

"You wanker." He laughs.

IT'S THE day to learn how to shoot a rifle. Jack is politely disbelieving that I've never done it, never shot any kind of weapon apart from the paintball gun I don't mention—"They have shooting ranges in the city, you know"—and is convinced that I should try it. It could come in handy, he says. I can't possibly think how, but I'm always willing to try something new.

Paul and I collect up some beer cans, of which there are plenty, and take them out into the backyard. Backyard is a bit of a misnomer, as it's so huge and there's nothing like a street frontage, but it's the part of the property near the house that's away from the road that leads there. We go out towards an old shed, not one that I saw on my arrival; there's still a roof on it, from what I can tell, but it doesn't look in good repair.

Paul continues on inside and drops his cans on the ground, so I follow suit. As my eyes adjust, I see small square bales of hay, piled three up, against one of the walls.

"We keep some of the surplus hay here." He pulls over an old wooden table and climbs on it, then tosses down two of the top bales. I pick one up to estimate how much it weighs: I'm guessing around twenty-five kilograms, comparing it to gym weights, although it's a lot more cumbersome than those. And itchier. Paul jumps down again and picks up the other one. His biceps and forearm muscles stand out, and I wonder if that's how he developed his musculature, farm work as a teenager.

Jack arrives with the rifle from the gun safe. He's grumbled a bit about it as an unnecessary piece of clueless city-slicker bureaucracy, but I gather he does actually keep it in there. Paul and I take the hay outside and rest it against one of the walls; then we go inside and get the table, one of us at each end, and carry it out to put in front of the bales. Once that's set up, all three of us collect the cans, and Jack constructs a triangle of them on the table, four along the bottom rising to one at the top. It looks a bit like a fairground activity, one of the sideshow alley tests of skill; rather, I think, it's the sideshow alley that tries to look like this.

"Okay, your first lesson," says Jack. "This is the trigger."

I don't roll my eyes. It probably all seems equally obvious to him, so explaining that doesn't seem any more ridiculous than anything else. Paul grins, possibly at my politely interested facial expression. Jack goes on to explain the rest of the weapon and then shows me how to hold it.

"There'll be recoil against your shoulder. You won't expect it, even though I'm telling you now. Hold it tight in place."

I nod, and hold it as I think I'm supposed to.

"Okay. You're ready to go."

That was much less in the way of instruction than I expected. Paintball preparation had taken a lot longer.

"You just have to keep focused on the target," says Paul.

"Okay."

They stand on either side of me and slightly behind as I raise the rifle. I look along the barrel, see the pyramid of cans; hesitate before pulling the trigger; shoot.

I don't expect the recoil.

I look, and see that I've missed. The cans are intact.

Jack takes the rifle back and readies it again. "Next try."

I repeat, and miss again. I'm starting to feel pretty embarrassed. I don't want to be just some city dandy to Paul's parents.

"Not to worry," says Jack. "Not everyone gets it straightaway."

I nod without looking at him.

"You have to keep looking at the cans," says Paul. "Your eyes look away just before you fire."

They do?

On my third try, I hit the bottom left can, and a spike of exhilaration goes through me. It was true—I had let my attention go in that second before squeezing the trigger, as if my brain had decided that it had all the visual information necessary and could go on to other things, thinking about dinner or the current book or what Paul's parents think of me. But that's not real focus.

The fourth time, after Paul's rebuilt the cans, I hit the bottom left one again; and the fifth.

"That's not bad," says Jack. "It's easier for someone to get good if they're consistent but off-centre, than if they're all over the place. I remember some of your friends," he says to Paul.

After I decide I've had enough Paul has a go, and shoots the top one three times in a row.

"Show-off," I say to him. He smiles.

BEFORE DINNER, Sam asks if I can help her put together her Lego. As I reach over to the box, I feel a strong twinge in my shoulder. I excuse myself to go to the bathroom and, taking off my shirt, have a look in the mirror. There's already a bruise starting to form. I'll take a photo of it later: a reminder of my butchness this trip.

Returning to the Lego, I do more directing this time rather than actual construction, which I think works well: Sam was really starting to get the hang of it with the *Scooby-Doo* kit, and she only needs a couple of corrections. Then there's a lot of flying the chariot around, sometimes with Xena in it and sometimes pursued by Xena.

"The baddies have kidnapped Gabrielle," says Sam. Gabrielle is a small plastic toy cat that she appears to have discovered somewhere and has placed precariously in the chariot. "You be the baddies."

I do a mwah-ha-ha laugh and raise the chariot up, making sure to use my left arm. I'm sitting on the ground, so Sam can just reach it. She lets out her war cry.

"That's quite a yodel," says Barb.

THE NEXT day we go back into Emerald. I actually had a look at Jack and Barb's computer, and the only problem was that the Wi-Fi was spotty throughout the house. They were talking about how they could change the layout of their devices around the house—they could move the desktop, but where it was now was a good room for it with the window, or maybe they could move the router, but that was limited in where it could be relocated, so on the other hand...—so I suggest that they just get a Wi-Fi extender, and I'll help them install it. I've installed a powerline Ethernet kit in my own house, and it wasn't hard.

"Really, we don't expect you to be doing this on a holiday," says Barb.

"I don't mind at all. I'll get to check out Emerald too." There's a playground that they take Sam to sometimes, so she's sold on the plan as well.

We get the Wi-Fi extender out of the way first, and then Barb asks if I'd prefer to go to the big newish Central Highlands Marketplace or the old main street to look around and then get something to eat. I choose the old main street, which turns out to be fairly quiet.

"It was really busy here a few years back, with all the mining," says Jack. "New utes everywhere, couldn't get a parking spot. That's all finished now." He points out the empty shopfronts: a former clothes shop, a former restaurant.

"A lot of guys a few years ahead of me at school came back here from Brisbane when the boom was in full swing," says Paul. "It was insane how much they were getting paid. One of them bought a Jet Ski to use on Fairbairn Dam. He didn't even have a trailer, so it just sat there." He shakes his head.

"And a lot of them have just gone again," says Barb. "There's not so many people you boys' age left here."

"There's still a few," says Paul. "There's a get-together on Saturday night at the O'Connell property, some of my friends. You should come," he says to me.

He obviously wants to go. "Sure."

"Can you stop talking now?" asks Sam.

"No." Paul glances down at her.

"Did you want to get anything from town?" Barb nudges my arm.

"A hat," I say. "A total country one. Like Lee Kernaghan." Jack and Paul have both worn old ones out on the property; there's a stash of them near the old boots.

"Are you sure?" Paul asks.

"Yep."

There is still a hat and boot store on the street that hasn't closed, so we go in. I resolve to be quick so that Sam's not too bored, and the salesman there seems happy to oblige. I walk out with a black country one that looked exactly like the photo I'd shown the salesman; Paul and Jack seem satisfied that it'll do the job. No inauthentic tourist rubbish, not that there'd be enough tourists coming here for such a thing to exist.

"Now how about Theo's for something to eat?" suggests Barb.

Sam has it confirmed that they have milkshakes, and we all agree: it's just across the street. The coffee turns out to be okay, and I'm glad to have one at last—back at the house I've been drinking tea, the "would you like a cuppa?" coming almost as frequently as "would you like a beer?"—and the food portions are enormous. I think I'll have a nap this afternoon. After the visit to the playground, of course.

I DO have a nap. Paul's gone for a walk with his dad, and Sam's playing with a box of old toys that appear to be kept for visiting grandchildren. Maybe toy Gabrielle came from there. I wonder which ones were Paul's.

Barb's in the kitchen, preparing dinner, so I join her and pick up a peeler.

"You don't have to do that."

"I'm on holiday, I know. But I like peeling potatoes." It's a baked dinner she's getting ready. "And topping and tailing beans. One of my hobbies."

She smiles. "All right, then."

As I'm peeling she says, "It's fairly quiet here this year. Normally Paul's brother and his wife would be here, and Paul's sister and her husband, but they had Christmas with their in-laws. You're not married, I suppose." I assume she's supposing that since I'm here by myself.

"No, not married. I probably spend too much time at work."

"With your computers."

"With my computers." I debate with myself, how open to be. Not to give anything away, of course. "My last relationship was a long-distance one, overseas. Didn't work out being so far away."

"Jack and I met at school and got married young. And since then the longest we've been apart is a week, when he was in hospital. He was kicked by a bull that time. The children were still small." She's looking out the kitchen window as she's talking. "I think Paul wanted the same thing. Got married young. Kaylee and Declan used to spend a lot of time here when they were growing up."

"Declan?"

"Kaylee's brother. Kaylee, that's Paul's ex-wife."

"I met her once." Sort of. I don't mention the raging argument. I've noticed that there are a lot of pictures around the house of Paul's siblings and their spouses, but of Paul and Kaylee there's only one. I guess Barb's taken most of them down to avoid them being reminders for Paul, but forgot the one that's in the back room, whose purpose now seems to be to store junk. I've gone in there a few times specifically to look at the photo. Paul's really young, only late teens, with a big grin; Kaylee is more serious, but definitely pretty, as I'd guessed from beneath her scowl that night. I think I'd recognize her now if I met her properly. I don't expect I will.

"It sounds like Paul spends a bit of time with you."

I startle. Every minute I can manage would be the accurate answer. What's she looking for? "I drop in to his place from time to time."

"He's told me about going out with you a few times too. How he saw Boney M." My heart's beating faster, and my mind's trying to think up ways to downplay, deny. She continues, "He seems like he's doing okay, but when I ask, all I get from him is a 'fine.' I can't tell from so far away."

My heart slows again, heading back towards its normal rate. It sounds like she's just feeling me out to see how he's coping after the split from Kaylee, using this time where there's just the two of us to pump me for information. "I think he is doing okay. He's got a decent amount of work lined up, he's renovating his house, and making progress with that, and he hangs out with some of my friends sometimes too for the social side of things, normal stuff like bands or footie in the park. So he's keeping occupied, and Sam seems to be doing fine too, making friends at preschool and vacation care pretty quickly."

She looks at me and laughs quietly. "That's almost more detail than I've ever had directly from him."

"I hope I haven't given away any state secrets."

"I won't tell."

AFTER DINNER and bedtime for Sam, we play five hundred and drink more tea. I haven't played before, but it's one of those games like bridge, with a few differences in the bidding and special cards and lack of a dummy; so I pick it up fairly quickly.

"It's good to have a fourth playing," says Barb, who's my partner. She's a sneaky player, and we're close to winning, thanks to her inspired guessing of what my imperfect bids mean.

"Thought this game might be a bit quiet for city folk," says Jack. I smile: it's taken several days before he's actually used the phrase "city folk" when referring to me. Maybe he's trying to put me off my game.

"I play bridge, which is pretty close."

"Hah, so you're a card shark," says Paul.

"I don't think it's me that's the shark," I say, looking at Barb. She just smiles and then plays the right bower.

I DO get some time just sitting by myself on the veranda, while the others are inspecting fences or looking over equipment or hanging out washing or riding a tricycle around in circles. It's just me and the wide brown land. It's beautiful in its way.

CHAPTER 10

"Do you know how to ride a horse?" Paul asks me as we're sitting on the veranda in the late-morning warmth, sipping from the tin pannikins used for outdoor tea drinking.

"I've ridden a couple of times." Just on backpacking holidays, years ago now.

"Want to go for a ride? Mum will look after Sam."

"Sounds good."

The two of us go out to the shed where the horses live. I decide to wear my new hat for the first time, to look as cowboyish as possible. Jack comes too, although he's going to stay at the house to wait for the vet to come: apparently a few of the cattle have what Jack thinks looks like wooden tongue, where—as the name suggests, he tells me—their tongues get stiff after an infection, from being scraped and abraded by dry sharp feed. But he helps us—rather, helps Paul, since I don't know what to do—saddle up two of the horses. Paul chooses one that he's ridden often before, and I get one that Jack assures me is fairly docile. Mine's black and fairly large, and his looks are the sort that in movies would indicate a bad-tempered beast, but I believe Jack.

Paul pretty much just jumps into the saddle, while my mounting is somewhat slower and assisted by a medium-height drum. But after that, we're off. Jack's right—my horse, jokingly named Killer, is very easy-going—and I'm not having any trouble at all.

As we're riding, horses side by side, Paul's pointing things out. "The Nogoa River's in that direction; over this other way you can see the land rising." It's not so flat there, with the occasional hillock. Trees are still fairly sparse, although on the hillocks there are clumps of them. "That's where we had a bullock go mad one year, attacking the cows. We had to shoot him. You'd be able to do that now." He smiles at me.

I envisage myself standing with a shaking gun as a one-tonne animal bears down on me. "Not a career I'm thinking of taking up."

The sun's hot—it's probably thirty-five degrees—and the flies are about, but I don't mind. I like riding out here with Paul. Hearing about where he grew up.

We're heading towards one of those clumps of trees, although this one isn't on a hillock. "We'll stop here for a bit," says Paul. It'll give me a chance to wipe some of the sweat off.

When we get in among the trees, Paul jumps down and tethers his horse and mine. Then he takes a blanket from his horse and strides off. I think to myself that he might have helped me down, but I want to show that I can do it myself, so I don't call him back for help. It doesn't take me too long, and after a sip from my now lukewarm water bottle and a few leg and back stretches, I follow the direction he's taken, although I can't see him through the trees.

After a short distance, the trees open up to a waterhole. And Paul is there lying on his horse blanket, naked. He would have only had a minute or three on me, but in that time he's stripped down and started playing with his cock. There hasn't been time for him to get hard, but he has his cock cupped in his right hand, squeezing it, and as I watch, it's growing. His eyes are closed, and he isn't paying attention to my presence. I watch until he's fully hard, and then I take off my hat and shirt and walk over to him, kneel between his spread legs, and start sucking.

His eyes stay closed, but he bucks his hips and his hands reach up until they find my head and they rest there. After he comes his eyes finally open and he looks at me. "Come on me," he says. It's only a matter of minutes before I oblige.

I lie down next to him on the blanket, and even though we're hot and sticky, he puts his arm behind my head, around my shoulder. "When I was a teenager this is where I used to come and wank. I could hear when the quad bike was coming, so I could just get naked out here and not worry. And the waterhole was handy for washing off afterwards. Sometimes I'd imagine someone stumbling onto my hidey-hole here—someone I never actually pictured, who somehow appeared on the farm—and somehow I wouldn't hear the quad bike—while I was in the middle of stroking myself, and y'know—"

"Basically doing what I did."

"Yeah. I wonder how things might have been different if it'd happened."

"If someone—presumably someone hot—had beamed down onto the farm and had their way with you."

"Yeah."

"If there'd been *Star Trek* teleporter technology, and—"

"Shut up." He looks at me, with the intense blue gaze I've only experienced the full force of a handful of times. "I'm glad you came here."

"I love you," I say. I don't intend to; it just slips out. I start thinking of how to do damage control. But he kisses me, and the kiss lasts for a long time, and miraculously I stop thinking.

SATURDAY EVENING at the house, Paul asks, "Do you mind driving? I'll probably have a few tonight."

"Sure."

He's wearing his trusty going-out outfit, and as always has scrubbed up well. I didn't have many options for what to wear, but after googling some country music singers, it seems like a plain black T-shirt shouldn't look out of place, even a fairly tight one, so it's that and jeans and boots. I don't wear my hat.

We say goodbye and an early goodnight to Sam, and then hop in the old ute. It turns out to be a column shift, so I tell Paul I'll need to do a couple of minutes' practice in the yard here: there probably won't be much need for gear changes, given the lack of traffic lights, but I like to be prepared. Late at night isn't the time to discover I don't know what I'm doing. Transition from first to second straightforward; reverse okay; all good. While I'm doing this, Paul's jiggling his knee, humming to himself—"Boys From The Bush," the song about boys piling in the ute on a Saturday night. I guess I'm an honorary one tonight. He doesn't seem impatient, just filled with a partially suppressed energy.

"Okay," I say, "off we go."

The kangaroos aren't so bad today, but I drive carefully when they're around anyway. Once we're on some fairly empty road, I ask, "Any idea who's going tonight?"

"Nah, we'd never really know. Just whoever turns up. It'd mostly be people from my old school, I reckon."

"Anyone close?"

He looks at me. "What?" The tone makes it, *What are you implying?*

"Like a best friend from school, or anything."

"Not really. There were a couple of blokes who'd come out to the property and we'd hang out, but they're not in Emerald now." And Kaylee and Declan.

Random people, here I come.

On the way, we stop at a bottle shop and buy a slab of beer. Since I'm driving, I'll be having two, leaving twenty-two for Paul and/or sharing. He won't drink twenty-two of them, will he? Maybe I'll be carrying him back to the ute.

At the O'Connell property, there are already a bunch of utes, and a few cars, parked. I smile to myself a bit: looking around at other arrivals, my imposture—wearing my black T-shirt, driving a ute, and carrying a slab—seems to be satisfactory. Paul's striding ahead, and goes into the house. He says hello to an older couple—Mr and Mrs O'Connell—and introduces me as a friend from down south, just visiting with his parents. Then we head out the back.

It's another giant backyard, although actually a yard here, this close in to town, rather than the arbitrarily nominated area of Paul's parents' place. It's still quite a distance until there's any connection to neighbours. Some large speakers have been set up for the music— some country stuff I don't know is playing at the moment—and tubs with ice for drinks. People who look to be mostly in their twenties are milling around.

We go to drop off the beer first, taking one each for ourselves. "We'll go find Greg first," says Paul. "It's his parents' place."

But we get waylaid looking for him, which turns out to be pretty much how the whole evening unfolds. We get stopped first by two couples, although I only catch the name of one of the guys, Dave. They manage to get a few words in with Paul until someone barrels in from the side and carries Paul along with him. I hear "Greg!" and then it's just me left with these four.

"So how do you know Paul?" asks the woman who appears to be with Dave, judging by the close body language. No wedding ring. I'll think of her as Dave's Girlfriend, DG.

"I live next door to him in Sydney," I say. "I'd never been to this part of the country so he invited me up to visit."

"Yeah, he always used to have people stay. You went shooting roos a few times, didn't you, Dave?"

Dave nods. "Yeah, we'd stay there the weekend sometimes."

"No roos for me. I'm still working on hitting cans."

"Gotta start somewhere," says Dave.

"Sydney. Isn't that where the shirtlifter went?" That's the other guy. I look at him and try to guess his story. He looks like he might have been athletic once, but he's not in good shape now, his neck and waist both thick, his pecs sagging; glancing over to see where Paul is, I note what good shape Paul's kept himself in compared to a lot of people here. This guy here was probably good at sports; maybe got himself a job in the mines; married, I see from the ring; had everything looking rosy once; now, from his slightly glazed and sour look, I guess he's sour about life. I'll dub him the Jerk. Of course I don't know if this is even slightly accurate, or fair, but I notice that the other three are frowning at him. I may have raised my eyebrows.

I wonder if the shirtlifter is a reference to Paul's former brother-in-law, or whether there's been more than one gay guy here of note.

"Could you get me another cruiser, babe?" says the remaining woman, who must be his wife: Jerk's Wife, JW. She can still dress to draw attention, and does. He grunts an acknowledgement and heads over to the ice buckets. With Jerk gone, JW turns her attention back to me, and it's more appraising.

"Lots of different people in Sydney," I say.

"Yeah, lots of reasons to live there," says Dave. "What do you do for a crust?"

"Computers."

"Computers, eh? I'm always having trouble with mine."

"Yeah, I work more with the data. I'm doing some work over in Los Angeles at the moment with the fire department there."

"LA," says JW, leaning forward. "Have you met any movie stars there?"

"Not really," I say. "Although the last time I was there, there was a guy I'd seen in a TV series that I got to meet." I take another drink of beer, and pretty transparently flex my bicep as I do; I see she notes it. I think my assessment of Jerk and JW—she now perhaps regretting the marriage to the soured, formerly fit guy—might not be too far from the mark.

Dave, however, is more interested in the fire service aspect of it. It turns out he's a volunteer firefighter, and really into it. I tell him what I can of what they do in LA, which isn't much, but he's still excited about it. DG occasionally gets a word in, but seems happy to let him go on about it; JW just watches me. I wonder where Jerk has gotten to, but don't mind that he hasn't returned. And then the conversation turns to the latest Star Wars movie, which Dave saw and loved; that's the point at which JW detaches herself, perhaps having decided to give up on me as a prospect for a quick pash in the shadows.

It's a shame that Dave and DG, whose name I never actually learn, have to leave early: I like them. When they go, I see that now Paul is talking to a woman with a few kids around her. I figure I've entertained myself for a while, so I can go and check in with him.

"Five is a difficult age," she's saying. "When they start school things change."

She looks older than me, a bit careworn—probably connected to the two children near her, the infant she's holding, and the large belly of pregnancy.

"This is Tracy," says Paul. "We were in the same class for years."
I revise my impression: younger than me, much more careworn.
"Aaron," he says to her by way of introduction.

"Hi," she says, without a great deal of enthusiasm. To be fair, I
think, enthusiasm's probably a rare commodity in her situation. Then
she turns her attention entirely back to Paul.

"Sam seems to be doing okay," Paul says. "She gets on at
preschool, although she's been in a couple of fights."

"You don't want that for a little girl," says Tracy. That gets my
back up a bit. I'm guessing the "fights" are just the roughhousing Sam
told me about with her sometime friend, sometime frenemy Finn;
nothing serious in my opinion, although I don't claim to be an expert.
Maybe Paul mentions it because he feels vulnerable about it, being a
single parent. "I'd say she needs more of a mother figure, with you
and Kaylee, you know."

That gets my back up further, and my sympathy for her diminishes.
I glance at my watch, 9.30 p.m.; I glance at the six-year-old, poking a
stick into a cage with a nervous-looking rabbit in it; I glance at the
three-year-old in an Elsa dress, asleep in a patch of mud at the back
of her mother's chair where ice has fallen onto the dust. *Who are you
to give parenting advice?* "Paul's been doing a pretty good job," I say.
Paul's quiet. *Let it go,* Elsa says to me in my mind; sounding super-
defensive would likely be unhelpful.

"You could get in touch with my sister Jessie," she says to Paul.
"She'd be happy to look after Sam when you need it now that she's
living in Sydney."

"Where in Sydney does she live?" I ask.

Tracy shrugs. "I'm sure it's not too far."

I finish my remaining half bottle and excuse myself to go to the
bathroom.

I circulate some more when I come back, this time with a can of
soft drink—I don't know whether they've run out of water or it's just
that nobody brought it in the first place. The people I talk to all fall
between Dave's enthusiasm and Tracy's and the Jerk's annoyingness

in terms of how likeable I find them. At about 11.00 p.m., I find Paul again, this time in a larger group.

I catch his attention. "I was thinking of heading off."

He's had quite a bit to drink by this stage and takes a few seconds to focus. "I reckon I might stay, eh."

Hmm, what to do? Should I stay and wait? He might want to crash here. That's probably the case, in fact, but maybe I'll double-check with the O'Connell parents on the way out. "Sure. Early flight for me tomorrow. Catch ya."

"See ya."

I find the O'Connells inside, on the way to drunk themselves, but still sober enough to assure me that the young people sleeping over here after one of these parties is standard practice, they don't mind at all, they love it in fact, they wish I could stay too. I make apologies for my early flight, thank them again, and head out.

I sit in the ute for a minute before I start it up. I'd fairly thoroughly considered the scenario where Paul was paralytic, and how I might get him back to his parents'. I'd also imagined another scenario where he was just frisky and we'd stopped by the side of the road on the way back for some time alone. Instead, I'm driving by myself.

When I get into the house, I leave a note on the kitchen table—Jack and Barb will be up before me—saying that Paul's stayed over, then brush my teeth and go to bed. I remonstrate with the voice of disappointment that's pointing out that Paul didn't want to come back with me: of course, these are friends of his from when he was growing up, who he hardly ever sees; of course, he should take the opportunity to catch up with them. *Don't be clingy*, I say to myself. *Don't be a jerk.*

I WAKE up just before my phone alarm and stuff my few things into my bag. I debate whether I should include the footie shorts Paul has loaned me. *I should wash them before I give them back*, I say to myself. Of course, that's not the actual reason I end up packing them. I can give them back in Sydney. When I go out for breakfast, everyone else is up.

"Where's Dad?" says Sam.

"Stayed at a friend's house last night," I say.

"You came back."

"He was seeing some old friends. Plus I have to catch a plane."

"When?"

"This morning."

"But I wanted to play Xena with you."

I wander over to get some Weet-Bix out of the pantry. "Sorry. We can play when you're back home. Have you had breakfast already?"

"She has," calls out Barb from just outside the door.

"Should I put a cuppa on for you?" I call back to Barb. It's funny how easy it is to slip into their speech rhythms after only a few days.

"Love one," she says. "One for Jack too if you wouldn't mind."

After the kettle's boiled and we're sitting around with our tea, Jack says, "You should come back again. There's more to see—we didn't get out to Fairbairn Dam at all."

"Or we could take a drive up north," says Barb.

"That sounds great," I say. It does. "I've really enjoyed being here." I have.

After we've started off in the ute, Sam sitting in her seat and me next to her, I ask her in a voice not meant to carry, "Have you had any fights at vacation care?"

"No."

"What about with Finn?"

"He's my friend again. I gave him my lollipop."

"That was nice. Did you say sorry too?"

"Yes."

"Good work."

"We'll pick up your dad on the way back from the airport, okay, Sam?" says Barb, turning around to look at us.

"Okay," says Sam.

AT THE airport I give Sam a farewell poke in the side, which makes her giggle. Jack and Barb get out of the car: Barb gives me a hug, and

Jack gives me a two-handed handshake, his left hand cupping the regular right-hand grip. I tell them again how much I enjoyed them having me there.

"You should come again, definitely. Or we might call in when we come to Sydney, if that's okay," says Jack.

"Sure. I'm the house on the left when you're facing Paul's. Any time." I give them my phone number too. They're still standing next to the ute, and Sam's waving through the window, as I enter the terminal.

CHAPTER 11

HOW'S IT hangin'? I text Paul the next day.

OK, I get back a couple of hours later. I wonder if he's still hung over. Then a short while after that, *How was your flight?*

It was a twenty-seater from Emerald to Brisbane, with more than the usual level of bumpiness. *Movie selection disappointing, otherwise good.* That ends up being the whole exchange.

I message again a couple of days later, a photo of me at work wearing my Emerald hat looking wistfully out the window. I get a smiley back.

Maybe he's busy, still catching up with people and doing things on the property. Maybe not. I think I shouldn't send another text, and I don't.

THE FOLLOWING day there's something unexpected. I'm back from work, although it's not too late in the evening, and I hear a knock at the door. It's a youngish guy, a few years younger than me, probably younger than Paul. He looks sort of familiar, but I can't place him.

"Can I help you?" I'm pretty sure he's not a missionary, unless the Mormons have ditched the white shirt and tie and gone with a slutty form-fitting look open halfway to the navel.

"Hi, I'm Kyle," he says. "I was looking for the electrician guy next door, he's done some work for me, and I just needed to get in touch with him." He puts his hands in his back pockets, which has the effect of pulling his jeans tight, or rather, tighter.

"He's not home now, but he has his phone with him."

"Yeah, um, I lost his number, but. Would you have it?"

"I do. Hang on." I get my phone from the table and come back. He's still standing there, hands still in pockets. "Do you want it?" It is Paul's work number, which is public, so I reassure myself it's okay to give it out.

"Oh, yeah." He takes his own phone out of one back pocket, letting his jeans relax to the extent that they can. As he's typing in the number, he says, "So do you know Paul well?" He looks up at me and smiles, then scowls as he notices he's pressed a wrong button on his phone.

What is this? Then it comes to me. It's Paul's former brother-in-law. Declan, not "Kyle" at all. The Queensland but, which sounds funny with the slight campness to the rest of his speech. His face is similar to his sister's, which I saw in the photo on the Emerald property and in person, with just that same scowl. How bizarre. What's he coming around for?

I shrug. "I know him to talk to. Have a beer with."

"I came past a few days ago and he wasn't here either. I think you were away too."

This is clearly a fishing expedition. What's the purpose? I recall Paul telling me, early on, how Declan had hit on him once. The flame has suddenly somehow rekindled, and Declan wants him again? But why would he be noticing that I hadn't been here? I'm guessing someone in Emerald mentioned that I'd been up there—obviously the bush telegraph is efficient. Maybe he wants to see who Paul invited there. Maybe he thinks that if there's something more going on than just neighbourliness, he'll have a chance with Paul: new city, new life. Maybe his sister put him up to it, thinks it will give her some leverage with Paul. Fortunately it's no difficulty to pretend there's nothing: it's a highly developed skill.

"Yeah, a couple of short Christmas trips. Nice relaxing holidays."

"Cool," he says. His hands are in his back pockets again, and this time, with his shoulders back, it has the additional effect of pulling his shirt farther open. He's smooth, twinky; I can see a nipple. He looks into my eyes. "This is probably a bit out of the blue, but would you like to get a coffee some time? Can I give you my number?"

I almost laugh; I do smile. "That is a bit out of the blue." I consider. If I get his number, it might help confirm that it really is Declan.

"Well, here it is." Fortuitously, he has it written down on a slip of paper. I take it.

"Thanks. No promises, though."

"A boy can hope." He laughs. Not my type, but he has a nice laugh—that at least seems genuine.

I GET home early evening the day Paul and Sam get back, and I drop over. Well, drop over—that sounds more casual than I actually feel. It's more going over to test the waters. Paul and Sam are at the table eating dinner.

"Hi!" says Sam.

"G'day," says Paul. "There's some pasta left, but no sauce."

"Okay." I go into the kitchen and put the remaining pasta into a bowl, then drizzle some olive oil over it.

"How was the rest of your holiday?" I sit down at the table.

"I got to ride on the quad bike again, in the trailer behind it I mean," says Sam.

"Cool."

They'd almost finished eating by the time I arrived, so I scoff the rest of mine, and the old routine—Paul organizing bath time and bed, me washing up—resumes. When I come into the lounge room, Paul's sitting in the sofa chair. I sit on the sofa, undoing my top shirt button, and sigh. I think about telling him about my day, but it wasn't very interesting, just tiring; and then I remember Kyle-Declan.

"Hey, you'll never guess. I had a random visitor at my door, and I'm pretty sure it was your ex-wife's brother, Declan, although he called himself Kyle." I go on and tell him what happened, and why I think it was Declan, describing what he looked like, his narrow face and prominent nose. I think it's kind of funny. Paul doesn't.

"You took his phone number?" he asks. "You practically announced you're gay."

"I guess." If he's local, he might have seen me around anyway and suspected that. "Here it is." I hand him the slip of paper. "I took it so you can ring him up if you want to find out whether it is him. You can always mention that was why I took it, that it was so you could get in contact with him."

He looks down at the floor. "Sorry." He stands up. "I guess I'm a bit tired from the long day, and I've got another early morning tomorrow."

I take the hint. "Okay. Have a good night."

At home I feel—disappointment. More than mere disappointment. I'd been looking forward to hanging out. To skin on skin. To things being as they had been, even though experience tells me that's just a vain hope. I contemplate the clouds on the horizon.

ON SATURDAY I'm going out for a ride, and a car pulls up and a woman gets out. She comes up to the gate. "Hi," she says. "Do you know if Paul lives next door?"

Perhaps I'm easily confused for a concierge service. "He does."

That's when he comes out. He stands there for a second.

"Paul!" she says.

"Jessie, hi. I see you've met my neighbour Aaron."

"Actually, we hadn't swapped names," she says. "Hi, Aaron."

"Hi, Jessie." From her appearance and her name, it has to be the sister of Tracy from Emerald. "Well, I was just off for a ride. Catch you later. Nice to meet you," I say to her.

I don't see Paul when I get back later that day; the house stays dark. Same on Sunday. I go for another ride then, longer.

IT'S DAYS later. I look out the window from my desk, and my doubts from the last days all coalesce. Paul's in the street with Jessie: his right hand is cupping her face, his thumb grazing her cheekbone. I get up from my chair and move away from the window, go and sit on the stairs, but shortly there's the expected knock. I open the door, and Paul comes in, just a few feet into the hallway.

"I've been doing some thinking since I came back from Queensland," he says.

I nod.

"I don't want to keep doing what we were doing. I want a normal life and I want Sam to have a mother. I'm going to ask Jessie out. I'm just here to get things straight with you before I do that."

Sam already has a mother, your ex-wife. "Okay."

"You had me thinking this was normal, what we fell into. Pulling me in with beach trips and jumping castles for Sam"—he's working himself up to that tight-voiced anger—"books and Greek stories, all that bullshit." *This is how he argues with his ex-wife*, I think to myself.

"Okay," I say. My voice is stable. "As far as everyone knows we're just neighbours, and that's how it will stay. It'll be as if nothing ever happened." Of course it won't be as if nothing ever happened; not for me. "Except I won't come over any more, of course. Is that all?" I put my hand on the door, the way I would for a departing guest, while at the same time keeping my distance from Paul.

He reads my body language. "Yeah." And then he leaves and I close the door.

I return to sitting on the stairs. *I'm smart*, I think to myself, *I have a good job, I own this house. I'm successful. So how am I so fucking stupid?* Fool me once—Trent did. Now it's shame on me.

It could have been worse. Was, with Trent, when he'd been seeing the woman he left me for for three months before I found out, three months where I'd thought he and I were together—at least when we could be—and keeping our secret from the world.

I can at least see Paul's worldview, even if I think it's totally wrong. But that's not something I could convince him about via intellectual debate: "You should stay with me because geopolitical trends are favouring the normalization of the nontraditional family." Not even me with my palm cards. And remembering the humiliating desperation with Trent—"Please, tell me what's wrong and how I can fix it," when all that would fix it was me not being male, me not being me—I couldn't bear to do that again.

I'm feeling fairly clearheaded at the moment, fully functional. I decide to take advantage of that while I still can. Make a plan. Because I know it will all go to shit soon. What plan can I dredge up?

I go and get my phone. "Howie?"

"Aaron, wassup?"

"I really need a favour, Howie. Really badly. You know the stuff in LA I've been doing—I have to go back there at really short notice, fix up this giant problem that's just come up. Like, maybe the end of next week." It's a lie, but by later it won't be. "It could be for six weeks, and you know I have this cat now, and I need someone to look after her. What do you reckon about coming to live with me? I mean, obviously we won't be living together while you're here and I'm in LA, but you could keep staying here after that too."

"Hey man, this is sudden." He sounds doubtful, understandably.

"I know, but I'm desperate." That's true. "I figured you don't like your current housemates. And having the party at my house the other week reminded me how much fun it was living with you." That's true too. "Please, man." My voice cracks, and I cough to cover it up.

"You're right, that was good."

"And you won't have to pay rent while you're housesitting, of course. Can you at least housesit while I'm away?"

"Yeah, I can do that. And y'know, the living together again is starting to sound good too. Just give me some time to think about it."

"Thanks, man. I really owe you. Now I have to get back to this work call that's caused all this hassle. I'll talk to you soon about how it'll all work."

"Sure, roomie. Heh. See ya."

I hang up. My mind is clear, but my traitorous body knows. The tidal wave of nausea has swept in and I rush to the bathroom, just in time.

IT'S A week and a half since everything changed, and I'm on a plane to LA. It was no effort at all to convince the company I should go: I can be a forward deployed embeddee for six weeks and be twice as productive as I could be in three two-week stints; even more if I work late, which I plan to do. The project will be a lot closer to completion after this.

Howie decided quickly and moved in two days before I left. I'd made a document for him with household information—where the vet is, which keys go with which doors and windows, how the PlayStation is hooked up to the TV. I also told him that I'd had a property dispute with Paul, so he shouldn't expect him to be as friendly as those times we'd all been out together; he might be standoffish, even. That all seemed to go smoothly enough.

Less smooth was a visit from Sam. She came in through the fence door one afternoon before Howie's arrival when I was sitting out in the backyard with Gabi.

"How come you don't come over? I ask Dad if we can come to your house but he says no."

"Lots of work," I'd said. "Grown-up stuff." I'd paused. I don't want her to get the impression that I've ditched her completely on account of my work, that she's less important than my work. "Also, your dad and I are kind of frenemies now."

"You didn't kick him, but."

"No, I didn't kick him. Anyway, I have to go overseas soon for a while—I won't even be back when you start at your new big school. While I'm away, my friend Howie will be living here, and it's cool with us if you still want to come and see Gabi. But it's up to your dad—he makes the rules for you."

She bent down and seemed to be trying to squeeze in all the cat-patting she could manage in the few minutes before she went back. At the gate she turned and gave me a small wave. "Bye."

I sat on the back step until my eyes were completely dry again.

While I can keep myself busy with work, keep my mind occupied, it's things like that that can sneak past my defences. And even when my mind is occupied and I'm not consciously aware of feelings, my body is. It was like that after the breakup with Trent—I was doing fine in classes, could focus, was glad to focus, but I threw up all the time. I lost ten kilos, and I'd been skinny enough to start with. No one knew; still, no one does; I'd promised I wouldn't tell anyone, and even though I thought Trent had been pretty crappy towards me, I still loved him and thought he might change his mind, come back, apologize, all those things a teenage mind will imagine; and regardless, a promise was a promise. That was when I moved in with Howie, and that helped, all unknowingly on his part.

It's time for a meal, nominally dinner. I'm sitting on an aisle seat, deliberately chosen, with a big guy to my right. As the trolley comes closer, I can smell at least one of the meals, chicken with a heavy sauce, getting stronger and stronger. Before the trolley gets to me, the nausea becomes unbearable, and I rush to the toilet.

CHAPTER 12

IT WAS a long six weeks in LA. Which was good. Distance was good. A month and a half of working until ten each night.

The taxi pulls up outside my place. I do experience a twinge—I hope Paul's not around—but it's all dark next door. I pay the driver, get my suitcase out of the boot, and unlock the door to my own house.

There's a light on in the kitchen, so I call out.

"Welcome back!" says Howie. He comes and gives me a bro hug. Gabi is in the kitchen too, and I think from her twisting around my legs that she remembers me.

"How's Gabi been? Any trouble?"

"No, she's been fine. It's all been quiet around here. No problems at all."

That's good.

"You hungry?" Howie asks.

"No, pretty much never after a flight. Maybe a cup of tea, though, before I go and have a shower."

He switches the kettle on. "You look tired."

"Yep. Fourteen hours."

"You look like you've lost weight, though."

"Maybe." I expect I have.

He comes over and squeezes my bicep. "Still muscle tone. Are you in training?"

"Thinking about it." Most evenings after work, after the ten o'clock finish, I'd go to the gym in my hotel. When I'd lost weight before—in particular that time post-Trent—it disappeared from my upper body first. Just left me skinny again. So I made sure to keep that up, the upper body weights; cycled, too, because it's my routine. It probably looks like I'm training for some cycling race. I'll have to look one up that I could plausibly be training for.

"You're about back to the weight you were when we first lived together and you cycled all the time then." Tried to cycle my problems away that time too.

Howie makes the tea, one for himself as well. "How's living here been?" I ask.

"It's been great being away from those arseholes from the last place, although I haven't spent too much time in the house here." Out with the modelling crew a lot, I guess, or the boozehound journalists. "It's a nice neighbourhood." He blows on the surface of the tea, takes a sip. "I've chatted to the little girl from next door, Sam. She's come through that gate you have in the back fence and played with Gabi. I haven't really seen Paul to talk to, though. He seems to be out a lot, and the couple of times I have seen him, he hasn't said much. What was it you said before you left? Standoffish, that was it. It's odd, because he was friendly all those times last year when we'd hang out."

I'm not up for a conversation about Paul. I shrug. If Howie doesn't stop, I'll just go and have a shower.

"Ah, there was a visitor for you while you were away. A gentleman caller." He smiles. "He didn't leave his name. And he looked a little nervous, dressed up and nervous. Very mysterious."

I shrug again.

"Speaking of gentleman suitors, did you see Xavier while you were in LA? Was it awkward?"

"No, I didn't see him at all. I think he was in New York the whole time." That was fortunate. It wouldn't have bothered me working with him, but I probably would have had to display some level of sociability to avoid an appearance of bad feelings, to make sure he didn't worry that he'd insulted me or hurt my feelings, and I didn't feel like that. "So it was all just work. How about you?"

"No romance here, but that's okay. I've thought about that conversation we had. Maybe we can have another house party, although I'm not planning to start picking your brain about it after you've only just gotten off the plane. I've mostly been hanging around with Sveta—

Ted hasn't been around much—and we've just been waiting for you to get back."

"It's nice to be missed." I toast him with the last mouthful of tea left in the mug, then go to freshen up.

Back in my room after the shower, I put on Everything But The Girl. It's the first time since things went bad with Paul. It was all too intense before, but now there's some distance. Not physical distance, of course—now that he's just next door again—but distance from the feelings. Now I'm back in the desert, and ready to start making my way back into the dry landscape ahead of me.

I'M SITTING out the back. The weather's cooled a bit, but it's still fairly warm; I can still sit outside in T-shirt and shorts as the sun's getting lower.

Sam comes through the gate.

"Hi Aaron," she says, as if I hadn't been away.

"Hi Sam. How's your new school?"

"It's okay. I have to wear a uniform now. Is Gabi still my cat?"

I take a second to adjust to the non sequitur.

"I said she was when we got her, so sure. Nothing's changed with that."

"Are you and my dad still frenemies?"

"I think so. I'm sad about it, and I miss coming and having dinner with you."

"Jessie comes instead. I don't really like her."

I think it would be unhelpful to continue this conversation. "Would you like a drink?"

"Yes please."

I get her some juice, and she moves on to playing with Gabi.

AT WORK I get thanked a lot: "It was great that you could get the whole project wrapped up in LA ahead of schedule, we ended up looking good," and the like. Dean comes around to my desk and talks about what we could do better, features we can add on, now that there's more time to think. Better algorithms we can design and roll out. He's excited, and I'm happy for him to ramble on, although I don't contribute much. He accepts my excuse that I'm a bit burnt out after the LA stint, and that I'll get back to talking about algorithms after a break.

I've been staying at work until after dinner time so that I don't run into Paul, and as a consequence barely seeing Howie before going to bed. But after pleading burnout I can't really hang around the office late with any justification, so I start going home earlier.

Early one evening, sitting at my desk while staring into space, I hear a child yelling. Not a sound of pain, more a massive tantrum. I see Sam being pulled from a car, red-faced, Paul holding her by the shoulders, then putting her under his arm. That kind of tantrum is something I'd expect from a two-year-old, not her. She's still yelling, but I can't make out any words.

The pang I feel at seeing Paul for the first time in months is muted, overlaid by wondering about what's going on with Sam.

A woman gets out of the driver's seat. "I'll call you later, Jessie," says Paul as he's pushing Sam through the door. Now I recognize her, from that one time she came past and asked for Paul before I went to LA; I notice again how she looks like a younger, fresher version of her sister from Emerald.

"I don't think he's a good influence," she calls out. She stands at her car door for a while, then gets in and drives away.

Who's not a good influence, I wonder. Is it me? It could be any number of males—some boy at school, some friend of Jessie's, Paul's father—but I think I'm a likely candidate. I wonder how much Sam's talked about how often I'd spent time over there, how her cat lives with me; things that would activate Jessie's warning senses.

I just want to go out now. Away from the house. After I get changed and head to the front door, Howie appears from his room. "I was going to make dinner. Should I make some for you?"

"Nah, I'm going out. Thanks, though."

I don't know where I'm going yet. Probably do a lot of walking, mixed in with bar-hopping. I don't want to pick up, but some mild flirting would be nice.

I'M WAITING for Sveta at the cafe; Axel's just come over to give me a long black and a hair ruffle. She's a bit late, which is uncharacteristic. She'd sent me a few texts while I was overseas, which was also unusual: we're usually fine to just do catch-ups in person, even after a long break. Her texts hadn't said much, and I'd been focused on work, so mine hadn't either. I sit and sip and ponder.

I think she looks a little drawn when she comes in. I wave her over, and Axel comes over too to take her order of a latte.

"You don't look great," she says. "Too thin."

"Neither do you." The best defence, et cetera.

"There's something I wanted to ask your advice about. You're my most clear-minded friend." Clear-eyed? Rational? Probably she means something like that.

"I was wondering just then if something was up."

"It's not new. Well, sort of, how big it is this time. It's Ted."

That makes sense. "Uh-huh."

"So I know that he hasn't always been faithful." That's news to me. He and I haven't ever talked about relationship matters; more about bridges. I suppose it's been clear I'm more Sveta's friend than his. "And I ignore it. But he has been seeing a secretary at his work, twenty years old, she is; seeing her for months. And he has gone away for a weekend with her."

"Wow. How did you find out?"

"I followed him to the airport."

"Not a work conference?"

"No, even though he said it was. I called the hotel, and there's no conference." She goes on to describe the conversation with the hotel clerk, and tailing Ted through the traffic. I wonder if she was wearing a trench coat and dark glasses.

"Good detective work there. What do you want to do?"

She shrugs. "I don't know. At my work one of our secretaries, part of a group I have coffee with sometimes, came in all tears. Her boyfriend had hooked up one night, and she came to coffee for sympathy. And it was all 'You should dump him' and 'Rip up his clothes and throw them on the streets.' For one hookup? It's normal for men. But this, with Ted's secretary, I don't know. Maybe too much."

"If you think it's just normal for men, you're basically giving him a licence to do what he wants. I mean, I wouldn't suggest dumping someone the first time that happens. But it's not true for all men, having some supposedly irresistible need to stray. I'm not like that."

"Perhaps you are strange. For a long time, I thought you just hid when you felt strongly and wanted something, but maybe you don't have the same urges."

She's probably right with the hiding; right too that I'm okay in my desert. Not at all right about how I feel—felt—with Paul, but we won't talk about that. "Well, Howie's not like that either, I'm pretty sure. He's a genuine guy. He'd just break up with someone instead of keep them as the second-string replacement, which is what it sounds like Ted is doing now. And that's pretty different from a one-night hookup."

Sveta makes a face that could mean doubtful agreement. "That is true. This is what I wanted, this argument, not just some fierce agreement that Ted is wicked." She pauses. "It would be a big step, moving out from Ted."

"It would. You have a good job, though, and friends. Not that I'm making any recommendations."

"No. I will decide. I do have a good job, yes. And friends."

If I hadn't asked Howie to move in, I would have volunteered to have Sveta stay. If she needs emergency accommodation, there is the room that's currently my office, but she probably won't: planning is her forte, and she seems as on top of things during today's crisis as she is at any other time.

Howie. As we drink our coffee, I start thinking about Howie. "You already know this, but just to say it out loud, you do deserve better," I say to her.

"FOUR NO-TRUMPS." It's a risky bid, but what does it matter? I'm forcing a slam, and my partner follows as he's supposed to, and then I have to play. I look at his hand when it goes down on the table: still risky. But I take a breath and play the hand quickly, hoping that either two finesses will work or my opponents will make a mistake.

Both hopes bear fruit, and I make the small slam.

"That was really good," says Gray, who was watching rather than playing himself. "Maybe you could give me some tips sometime."

There are some knowing looks exchanged among the other players. Great. Lance, as host, decides it's time to bring over more wine; he hands a glass to Gray. Thanks a lot, Lance.

Later I give Gray my number.

WE'VE ARRANGED to go to a small bar, Gray and I; I suggested the place. It's not too far from my house, so Gray comes to my place first. He's wearing a short-sleeved shirt, with the sleeves folded up; he has a tattoo on the inside of his left bicep, which is unexpected. He seems like a quiet guy, so maybe this is a kind of expression of daring, a look-I-can-be-bad statement. I sigh inside. I'm not really into tattoos making look-I-can-be-bad statements. But maybe I'm wrong, and anyway I don't want to start off the evening by being judgmental or hypercritical. I'm just about to suggest we head off when Howie comes to the door.

"You'll be out for dinner?" he asks.

"Yeah, we'll be grabbing something. Gray, this is my housemate Howie. Howie, Gray." Gray looks dazzled by Howie. Howie's just dressed in old clothes—ripped T-shirt, cut-off track pants—but pretty much nothing can obscure how good-looking he is.

"Nice to meet you," says Howie, shaking Gray's hand. Gray's still wordless.

As we walk along the street, Gray asks, "Howie's just a friend of yours?"

"Yes, since uni. A while ago now."

"Where does he come from?"

He's surprised that it's country NSW.

"He looks so exotic, though. I mean, he could be a model."

"Funnily, he is a model. Only part-time, though."

"Really? What kind of model? Underwear?"

Not for the first time, I think that I should delay introducing guys to Howie. The ones I intend to explore a relationship with, anyway. I'm not putting Gray in that category. Not yet. We'll see. "He's done some underwear campaigns, but regular clothes too."

He chatters more about Howie until we get to the bar.

At the bar, I order a glass of shiraz, and Gray orders a cosmopolitan. With his arm resting on the counter, I can see the tattoo more clearly. I'm fairly certain it says *Amor Vincit Omnia*. I decide to ask him about it, in part to change the topic from Howie.

"The tattoo, did you get that from Virgil?"

"Who?"

"Virgil. He wrote the *Eclogues*. The quote's from one of them, the last one I think."

"I'm not much of a reader."

I sigh again, still internally. As soon as it was out of my mouth I realized it was unlikely that it came from Virgil, worse that it was such a dorky question; it was more likely to have come from a book of quotes or the tattooist's samples. But the not-a-reader admission: can I get past that? Maybe I'd be shutting myself off from something good. Not that I want a relationship now. But getting to know Gray better could be worth it. He likes me, so that's something. You can't always know when you'll like someone, and the checklist approach isn't necessarily a good predictor. Paul isn't someone I would have predicted liking if I hadn't been his neighbour. True, he did like books, and he was thoughtful, at least before; and physically… there's the whole nonrational aspect to a feeling of simpatico, that feeling of simpatico I had once with Paul but that's now gone. Maybe I'd just imagined that feeling.

This is not the time to be thinking about Paul.

I don't think there's any point in asking whether the tattoo inspiration came from Caravaggio's painting either.

So we talk about work—Gray works in accounts at a bank—and then Star Wars. Inside I give thanks that Star Wars was such a universal hit: handy in case of faltering conversation.

I also mention Xavier.

"I thought you'd broken up on an earlier trip, just when I started at bridge."

"It's kind of complicated." Gray knows I was just in LA again, so I let him draw the inference. The essence of it is true, the unreadiness for a relationship, even if the detail isn't. I wouldn't mind hanging out with Gray again, even if there hasn't been a spark, but I really don't want to get into anything too quickly. No sex—my libido's in a state of torpor, like an arid-zone echidna—I'll just stay in my desert.

After I've kissed Gray goodnight on my doorstep—a fairly chaste kiss—I find Howie still up.

"I thought you might be having a guest."

"Nah."

"Think you'll see him again?"

"Probably. He'll probably want to check you out again anyway."

"What?"

"Next time maybe you can wear a paper bag over your head, if you haven't come down with some disfiguring illness."

He laughs. "Sorry."

"That's okay."

CHAPTER 13

IT'S A Saturday morning, and I'm on my way to do some grocery shopping, pulling along the granny cart with tote bags behind me. I'm just looking at the trees—more staring into space, really—when someone touches me on the elbow, startling me. I turn, and it's Declan. Paul's former brother-in-law.

"Hi there," he says. "Remember me?"

"I do. Kyle. Hi." I emphasize the name. I'm not sure what I'm feeling. It's not anything like dislike, but I don't especially want to talk to him. Don't want to talk to anyone, I suppose.

"Uh, yeah. Hey, do you feel like grabbing a coffee?"

No, I don't.

"Please?" he says, possibly noticing the expression on my face. "There's something I wanted to get off my chest."

I know what it is. Today he's not wearing his seduction outfit, just a Britney Spears T-shirt, with her larger-than-life-size face centred between his pecs. He looks normal. A normal gay guy.

"Is the something you want to get off your chest Britney?"

He looks confused, then laughs at my weak joke. "Nah, I like her there." He pats his chest.

I give in. "Okay, coffee."

He turns and waves to a small group of people sitting on the grass—maybe friends he came to the park with—and we go in to the nearest cafe, not one of my regular haunts, me pulling the cart behind me. Either it's not too popular or it's before the morning crowd.

"Long black," I order when the waitress comes over. Declan orders a latte.

"So," I say, "there was something you wanted to get off your chest that wasn't Britney Spears. Declan."

140

His face goes a deep red. "I'm really embarrassed. My sister—how much do you know?"

"Not much. I suppose you know I spent a few days up in Emerald after Christmas." He nods. "Paul's parents had mentioned you, and there was a photo there with you in it." There wasn't, not that I was aware of, but that's a concise story to explain how I recognize him, one that doesn't involve mentioning discussions with Paul.

"They did?" He seems surprised that Paul's parents had talked about him.

"Yeah. They said you were out on their property pretty often when you were younger."

"That's true. You know my sister and Paul were married, right?"

I nod.

"They were friends first. I was two years younger, so I'd tag along. We'd just hang around there a lot, go riding or whatever."

I don't want to hear him reminisce. "So what did your sister want that led you to being Kyle?"

"It wasn't a completely amicable split. Paul can be a bit, mmm, closed. And some things made her wonder—well, she heard about you visiting Emerald, and she thought that maybe you were gay."

"She thought right."

"And she wondered—"

How much of it has been her wondering, and how much Declan's? "She wondered wrong." I dislike direct lying, but I can do it. "He was just being neighbourly inviting me up there, the way you country folk are."

He smiles and shrugs. "Yeah, I know it doesn't have to mean anything. Anyway, she suggested I could pretend to be a customer of Paul's and go and check you out while he was still in Queensland."

"Okay, you've now checked me out."

"Not completely," he says, looking over the table at my body, and then blushes. That was so awkward, it's kind of cute. "You know," he says in a rush, "it's still surprising that Paul invited you. He was kind of—he had the typical attitude about gay people. He must have adjusted pretty quickly once he moved here."

"I guess he must have."

He pauses for a few seconds. "Did you see much of the property?"

"A bit. We rode around on the quad bike and on horses."

"Once—" He pauses again. "I went out on a horse, once. Just myself. I thought Paul was with Kaylee. But I found him—I don't think he saw me—he was, was—well, naked, and I thought—anyway, I left. But later, when I thought about it again, I wondered if it was a kind of—invitation. And he was really hot." I know. "It all went bad after that. When I said something. That was when I left and came to Sydney. I couldn't face how Paul felt."

That's amazingly confessional for a first proper conversation with someone. On the other hand, maybe I happen to be just the right audience. Sydney gay guys, his friends now, wouldn't know Paul, probably wouldn't know what it was like growing up in the country. People who knew Paul, people from Emerald, he wouldn't be telling them—his sister, especially. I could imagine the limited outlets he would have had up there, how seeing Paul naked would have been something he replayed in his mind over and over.

I ruthlessly push down the images in my own mind. I can't think about that again.

I feel sympathetic towards Declan. It must have been difficult. I'd still like to think that if I'd been in his situation, I wouldn't have hit on my sister's boyfriend, but it's pretty human.

"I can imagine," I say. "I think Paul's still not at Sydney levels of comfort. We're not really close." In my head I laugh a bitter laugh. "So what did you do when you got to Sydney? How did you find moving here?"

"It was a bit like coming home." I think he'd be quite at home at the Imperial. "I work in retail, so it was pretty easy getting a job." He names a clothes shop I know. We go on to talk about clothes and pop divas. I don't mind.

I'M STILL lying in bed on a Sunday morning when Howie comes past my door. "It's time for another house party, don't you reckon?" His tone's enthusiastic. "We could do it bigger than the last one. Maybe we could actually brew some beer for this one. I found this place where we can go and do it ourselves."

I sigh. It's not intentional. I'm just thinking about what will be involved, and how much I'll end up doing. I still have no motivation, so the preparation will be an enormous chore; and for the party itself, I imagine I'll be pretty flat, personality-wise. I guess I can busy myself with barbecuing and organizing.

Howie is frowning, annoyed. "You know, this wasn't what I imagined when I came to live with you. Maybe a sense of nostalgia has clouded my memory, but I'm sure it wasn't like this before. You used to want to have meals with me occasionally, and do fun stuff."

He's right. I haven't been eating with him, haven't been spending much time with him at all, although it's more for lack of appetite and just wanting to be alone. I'll try harder. I think it's time for some truth as well. Just some; a partial truth.

I pat the right side of the bed. "I'm sorry. Something happened that I haven't told you about." He comes and sits.

"Actually," I continue, "it was like this when we first started living together. I was pretty quiet then. And it was because I'd just broken up with someone." I figure that the statute of limitations for talking about Trent is well and truly up: no one I know has seen him or heard of him for years now.

Howie's look of annoyance vanishes. "I do remember that. I figured that you were just shy. I mean, you weren't before we lived together, which was why I thought it would be fun. But there was that period when it seemed like you were going out of your way to avoid me in the house." He laughs and colours slightly. "Now for my confession—I thought maybe you were keen on me and it was making things awkward."

I laugh too. "Did you really think that? I had no idea."

"Yeah, well. It didn't bother me. Anyway, who was it?"

"You remember Trent?"

"Of course I remember him. He kind of disappeared from our group—ah. You know, I hadn't guessed. I used to hang out with him at the bar, scoping out the uni chicks."

"Yeah."

"And then he got married, really young. Somewhere out of state, with mostly just his family and hers there. Almost none of us went."

"Yeah."

"Ah."

I tell him about high school, the sneaking around; uni, and more sneaking around. That I didn't mind it at the time, but that it isolated me more than I realized.

"I can believe it. Who'd you tell? I don't remember anyone else you were especially close to at the time. But then again, I didn't notice you and Trent either."

"No one. I promised I wouldn't."

"Until when?"

"Until now."

"Like, no one, no one."

"That's right."

"Huh." He looks me in the eyes. He's really very handsome. "Thanks for telling me."

"Which leads me to my actual point. The same thing happened again, sort of."

"Bummer. Anyone I know?"

Now's the time for the truth to stop. "No. But it's why I've been a bit mopey, I guess, and why I will be for a while."

"Aww." He lies down next to me and puts his arm across my chest. "We don't have to have a party."

"Sure, we can. It'll get me out of my funk." I doubt it, but it's better than sitting around.

He grips my shoulder and lies there for a while longer. Then he says, "Are you getting a hard-on?"

"Bugger off." I am, a bit. I'm still wearing just the boxers I slept in, so his skin is across my skin. That reminds me of what I miss, and that in turn kills the half boner.

He laughs. I decide it's time to redirect his attention.

"So there was something else I was going to talk to you about too."

"Yeah?"

"Sveta. And you. Did you ever think about going out with her?"

"Nah. Well, I mean, sort of. But she didn't like me when we first met, and then we kind of friend-zoned."

I could mention Sveta's meeting Paul, how she started off all combative with him but came to like him; but I don't want to talk about Paul, especially not just after I've been talking about my doomed relationship. Don't give extra chances for him to put two and two together. "You know, after you met her there was hardly any time where you didn't have a girlfriend. And she met Ted, and got stuck with him."

"Stuck?"

"I don't think things are very solid between them at the moment. Or will be in the future." She's told me she's decided to move out, and has already found a place, which is amazingly quick. She doesn't typically change her mind once she's settled on a course of action, even when it's a pretty major decision like this one. I'll leave it up to her to decide how much she wants to spill.

"Huh. I always figured she was good at understanding people and what they wanted. Knew that Ted was what she wanted. They've been together a long time now."

"Maybe she was wrong. I think Ted's not the guy for her."

"Maybe. You know, she wondered if there was something between you and Paul."

"Did she? Well, we just established how she can be wrong."

"True."

DEELIE COMES up the following weekend. Her birthday's coming up, so she's invited herself to fly up and stay with me. I'd normally be the one to suggest something like that, but it's the sort of thing that's just been slipping by me recently. I haven't even bought her a birthday present yet. Her imminent arrival kicks me into gear.

As her present, I decide to take her to the opera *Lakmé*, which is what's on this month. I have a moment of doubt—it's tragic, and worse, a tragedy about love—but we both like it, I don't have any other ideas, and I've pretty much run out of time. I'm a hopeless brother right now.

After I've booked the tickets, I think I should have gone for indoor skydiving. All adrenaline, no emotion. So I book that too.

She arrives on a late flight on the Friday, so it's pretty much time for bed after I've picked her up at the airport. She's sleeping on the pull-out sofa in the office.

The next morning, we have breakfast with Howie. He ruffles her hair when he comes into the kitchen. "Hey, kid." He's known her since she was small, before she and my parents moved to Melbourne when she started high school.

She makes a low growl in her throat and he laughs. He knows she gets mock-irritated when he does that to her hair. "I'm glad not all Aaron's friends are as annoying as you."

"What are you guys up to today?"

"Indoor skydiving, then *Lakmé*," she says.

"Skydiving? Why didn't you invite me?"

It's only because I did it all in a rush and didn't think. "It's for Deelie's birthday. I'll take you on your birthday."

"Happy birthday, kid! How old are you now? Nine?"

She growls again.

"What's lakmay? Some other weird sport?"

"An opera."

"Okay, you don't have to include me in that."

There's a longish drive out to the indoor skydiving place. When we're almost there, Deelie says, "You know, you're not your usual enthusiastically dorky self."

I shrug. "Tired, I guess." It's funny that this time seems worse than with Trent. Then, I'm pretty sure no one guessed. Maybe because the people who've come close to suspecting this time—well, person: Sveta, from what Howie said—I've known for more than a decade now, and there was no one like that then; and Deelie was only small.

But as well as there being people who know me better now, it feels like it's all just leaking out this time, my feelings, in a way I'd thought I could prevent. Could hide all traces of.

Fortunately at the skydiving, there's a bunch of stuff we have to do that keeps us occupied there: a half-hour's training, and getting changed into overalls and helmets, and watching another session before us. Then it's our turn: we're taken into the outer part of the main tube, a large multistorey clear vertical tunnel, where a giant fan blows air up through a netting floor. It's loud.

I'm second up. I go to stand in the doorway to the main part of the tube, and the instructor inside the tube grabs me and lowers me to be horizontal, about the height of his waist, although I bob around a bit and bump into the wall. But I'm floating. My stomach gives a lurch. Probably a good idea to have had just the toast for breakfast. And then the fan gets turned up higher, and I start rising. The instructor grips the sleeves of my overalls and, using some trick I can't quite work out, flips himself from vertical to horizontal, and we soar up the tube. My stomach lurches again, but it's fantastic.

Deelie's more of a natural at it than I am, less bumping into walls and floors. When she comes back out of the tube, her face is shining. I probably look like that too.

In spite of the temptation, I don't book another one. The adrenaline is saying, *Do it!* But I know it's just the rush. I probably will do it again; will take Howie. I'll make the decision when I'm rational again.

The drive back is fun, the way things usually are between us. The adrenaline's still there. I must remember that as a useful trick: when a relationship's made you mopey, and you're painful to be around, do something where your body tells you there's a danger of dying and you'll feel alive again.

The evening's good too. Deelie's brought up a dress to go to the opera, and I wear black tie—not at all necessary for the opera here, but it's fun to get dressed up. Howie whistles as we leave, and Deelie looks a bit embarrassed.

It's a good performance. Deelie and I both like the "Flower Duet," which Lakmé and her servant Mallika sing while collecting flowers. It's near the beginning, and nothing tragic has happened by this stage, but the music is really affecting. I look at Deelie, and her eyes seem bright. I wonder whether the opera will resonate with events in her life; whether she has a romantic life yet. I wonder about her former BFF Danielle, and whether there was any sapphic element to their friendship. As the story plays out, though, I know I can't ask her, not this visit: it gets to me as I was afraid it would, when Gerald chooses his regular life—for him, his regiment—over Lakmé, and Lakmé kills herself in unrequited love.

As we're walking out, I say, "Powerful stuff."

Deelie nods.

Neither of us feels like talking more.

THE NEXT morning Deelie's up before I am. She's made herself a coffee and is sitting in the backyard. I join her with my own coffee.

"I met the girl from next door. Sam."

"Did you?"

"Yeah. Seems like a good kid. She was just playing with Gabi." Gabi appears to have wandered off; I can't see her.

"She's the one who likes *Xena*."

"I remembered you telling me. She said you used to watch it with her a lot, but you don't anymore."

The other difference about keeping secrets now compared to with Trent—apart from decade-long friendships and teenage sisters—is having a talkative five-year-old neighbour.

"*Xena* had to give way to that big LA trip."

CHAPTER 14

THERE'S A knock at the front door the next Friday night. Howie won't be home until late, so I suppose I'd better answer it.

Jack's standing on the front step, Barb behind him. I stare, then pull up a smile. "You're in Sydney. Nice to see you." I shake Jack's hand, give Barb a hug.

"Just pulled in now." I see their ute parked along the street.

"You drove?"

"Yep. Made good time too."

"Would you like to come in?" Then I pause. "You'd be wanting to see Paul."

"He's not home; we've tried his house already."

Out with Jessie, I'm sure.

"Have you called?"

"Not yet. It was going to be a surprise," says Barb.

"It's a surprise," I say.

"I'll call him now." She steps back onto the footpath, but we can still hear clearly, at least her half of it.

"Not bad—we're outside your house—yes, your house—no, just planned to drop in for a few days—don't worry—no, really— we'll keep ourselves busy." She hangs up, comes back.

"Where's Campbelltown?" she asks.

"If you'd been going further south and had skirted Sydney, it'd be on the motorway just on the edge of the city, to the southwest. Probably an hour and a half from here."

"Okay," she says. "He's having dinner at the moment, and I told him he shouldn't worry about leaving straight away." She looks at me. "Where'd be good for dinner around here? It doesn't have to be fancy."

I could just give them directions to the main road, with its extensive selection of restaurants, I think. Let them explore by themselves. No one would expect me to take them to dinner, if they knew the circumstances. Not that anyone does.

"Come inside," I say. "Have a drink, then I'll take you somewhere. Cuppa?"

"Love one," they say together.

I EXCUSE myself to take a shower while they're having their tea. I don't really need one, but I can probably only manage enough conversation to last dinner and not many minutes more.

"Pick something unusual," says Jack as we're walking down the street.

I consider. "How about Ethiopian? You can eat the plates."

"That'd save washing up." That makes me think of Paul and having dinner at his house, and the old routine of washing up while Sam was being put to bed. It had been beginning to feel distant, fortunately, something from a different life, the LA trip having served its purpose of delineating my foolish before-life from my once-again-functioning now-life; but having Jack and Barb here has brought it back sharply. I think more about what we can talk about during dinner.

The Ethiopian restaurant is one of the closer ones, intentionally, so it's only ten minutes before we're there. We're seated and order beers, which arrive quickly, with just enough time before that to explain to them the way you eat with your hands here.

"Cheers." I clink glasses with them. "It's great to see you." It is nice to see them. All I need to do is divorce their presence from any memories of Paul.

"You look a bit tired," says Barb.

"Work," I say.

"Your computers."

"My computers."

Ready topic number one. "Travel too, across the Pacific to LA. Have you been following the Trans-Pacific Partnership talks?" I ask. It's a weak topic, but I haven't had long to prepare.

Of course Jack has been following it. He's in favour of the prospect of liberalization of agricultural trade, although it's not as extensive as it's usually portrayed. I talk about intellectual property issues, which is something he's thought of as rather airy-fairy; I give him a couple of examples where it matters in my work, which makes him nod, thoughtfully. We talk a bit about my work as well, including the fire department connection which interested Dave up in Emerald—it hadn't occurred to me that that might have been of interest to anyone before that evening—and it interests Jack and Barb too. All Paul-free conversation.

I can do this.

We order our food, and more beers.

They like the food: we'd ordered goat—"We could shoot some feral ones and cook them up, eh, Barb"—and some different vegetable dishes. They're good about trying things, really. The main courses are done, and we're finishing up with dessert and coffee and whiskey.

"I just remembered something we were going to ask you, Aaron," says Barb. "We'd taken some photos of when you were up in Emerald, but somehow we lost them."

"My fault," interjects Jack, "I thought I'd transferred them to the computer, but I did something or other wrong."

"We'd like to have some," continues Barb. I've seen how they print out ones of the grandkids and stick them on the fridge. "Do you reckon you could share some of yours with us? I remember you took some on your phone."

"Sure," I say, and hand it over.

That brings me back to the TPP, and the likely effect on technology imports; I'm thinking of phones and cameras, while Jack's thinking more of heavy machinery. I've had a number of beers. I've stopped worrying about everything—we're kind of in a groove here, I think, Jack and Barb and I, it's all easy, although part of me knows that it's the alcohol that's blurred my discomfort. *But that's what it's supposed to do*, I remind myself. *Shupposhed to*, I make my mental voice say. Heh. It lets me glide along with only my liking of Jack and Barb to the fore.

"You look happy in these photos," Barb is saying. "You all do."

She's flicked through all the Emerald photos—Sam playing on the trike and laughing wildly, a selfie of me riding the horse, another selfie of me with the rifle bruise on my shoulder, a photo of us all in the Emerald main street taken by a friend of Barb's, more—and she's on to older ones. Right now she's flicking past a photo I'd taken of Paul cooking in the kitchen with beer and spatula, to one taken of the three of us eating dinner at his place, Paul and Sam and I laughing at Sam having gotten pasta sauce in her hair, to the one of Paul at the beach, where he's wearing my swimmers and posing and grinning at me.

The alcohol high disappears in a flash, although its other effects don't. The haze of slow reaction still interferes with any sensible response.

"I was," I say. And I think, *Fuck. Fuck fuck fuck*. No dick pic on there could have been more revealing. Fuck.

And then I'm saved by Barb's phone. Not saved. It's too late to be saved. But at least I don't have to say anything right now.

It's Paul, of course. He's telling Barb that he's close to home and wondering where they are. I take back my phone that Barb's left on the table and check the time. It's later than I'd expected. I go up to the counter and pay, to avoid any arguments about who'll get the bill.

When I get back, I say, "It sounds like we should head back so you can see Paul and Sam."

"It's been lovely, this evening," says Barb.

"Absolutely," says Jack. "You really should come up to Emerald again."

"It would be great to go there again." It would, but it won't happen.

We walk home, and they're quite mellow. I don't think they notice that I'm not. When we're outside my house, Jack says, "Will you come in?"

"I think my housemate's home now, and there was something I wanted to sort out with him, so I'll let you catch up with Paul and Sam. I'll send photos."

I hug Barb and shake Jack's hand. I wonder if I'll see them again.

APART FROM Jack and Barb's visit, things have been going okay. I've been making more of an effort, eating dinner with Howie and just being around. Dinners have been mostly chicken breast with brown rice and greens, a staple for Howie; for me it's good for regaining muscle—I'm almost back to normal—and it's too bland to turn me off. I've seen Gray a few more times, at bridge and outside of it, although there haven't been any developments on that front. Work's going along okay. I have a routine again.

One surprise appears on a Friday night: Declan, at the door. I hadn't expected to see him again after he got his confession off his chest.

"I was just going out with some mates to the Imperial, and I thought, maybe Aaron would want to come. How about it?" He's wearing his seduction shirt from that first appearance, when he came to my door as Kyle, but this time it's only unbuttoned to the second button.

I think about it for a second. "Sure." It'll be the drag shows. "Come in. I'll just need to get changed. Take me about ten minutes."

"Quick change."

"Don't expect much." I get him a glass of water and sit him down.

As I'm going to my room, I call out to Howie. "I'm going out with a friend, Declan. He's just waiting while I get changed." Howie sticks his head out of his room. "Actually," I continue, "do you want to come? Drag show at the Imperial. I said I'd be ready in ten."

"I can do that."

I put on a black T-shirt and blue jeans, a low-effort outfit. The shirt is almost back to being form-fitting again, not flapping around my body. Howie's wearing a red T-shirt with white piping; as usual, he puts me in the shade, but it doesn't matter.

When we're in the lounge room, I say to Declan, "I invited my housemate, Howie, since you said it's a bunch of your friends."

"Of course. The more the merrier."

As we're walking along the street, Howie whispers to me, "So this was your gentleman caller while you were away. He didn't leave his name then." I can understand why.

At the Imperial, there's a group of five of Declan's friends already there. They look over when we arrive, and a couple of them giggle. I hear a loud oh-em-gee accompanying glances at Howie. The usual. It's not much later that the drag show starts. The first act is "It's Raining Men," and there's a lot of jumping around and singing along by the crowd. One of Declan's friends sings the word "Hallelujah" at Howie. I'll apologize to him later.

Between songs Declan says, "Most of tonight is Britney-themed, so I'm going to be a big dork about it. I hope that's okay."

I laugh and comment that this might be one of those times I need to run and hide; he laughs too at the Britney song reference.

The Britney marathon is okay, even though it's not really my thing. The acts start with older stuff, so there's some "Baby One More Time"—complete with drag queen in schoolgirl outfit—and "Oops!... I Did It Again." The boppiness is broken up by "From the Bottom of My Broken Heart." To my embarrassment, I find the lyrics affecting. They're worse than a country and western song, maudlin and banal, but I can't help but hear them. I'm sure I'll laugh about this one day, being moved by a Britney song. Not today, though.

Fortunately, they move back on to up-tempo songs. The next one is "Sometimes." Declan, standing in front of me, turns around and smiles. He has a nice smile. He sings along and dances a bit— more a wriggle than a dance, since the place is packed—and the brushing up against me, obviously not entirely accidental, warms me in a way I haven't felt in a while. I also notice that unlike his friends, Declan hasn't been paying any attention to Howie, beyond general politeness; just to me.

It would all turn into a ridiculous shambles if I were to do anything about this. I won't. I have an urge to put my arms around Declan, pull him closer, but I won't. It's not how it was with Paul—this feels more like a pilot light than full-blown heat, more a spray of water than an ocean wave, but it's nice to know that it's still possible for it to happen.

I decide to leave after the next song. I give Declan a hug and, this time, my phone number. Nothing will happen—I'll make sure of that—but he's a nice guy.

As we walk home, Howie puts his arm around my shoulders. "No invitation back home tonight either?"

"Nope."

"You could have. I saw that dancing."

"You could have too, an entire harem."

"Not my thing."

"A Britney-singing harem."

He laughs. "They were pretty over the top. Not Declan, though."

"Nah, he was okay."

Back in my bed, I jerk off and—not counting a handful of wet dreams—come for the first time since before I went to LA.

THE NEXT day I hear banging on the front door, loud and angry-sounding. It had been too much to hope that the uncomfortable accommodation we'd come to could hold, I suppose, without anything coming along to disrupt the fragile balance. My fragile balance.

I go and open the door before Howie can go to see what the noise is. It's Paul, of course. He comes into the hallway just as he did that last time.

"What are you playing at?" he says, already having worked himself up. I don't have any clue what he's talking about until he continues. "Hanging around with my parents, hanging around with Declan, doing, saying who knows what. You've obviously moved on, some new guy and all, so what do you want? Why are you doing it?"

The unjustness of it all is what gets to me. "I kept your parents occupied that one time they visited because you weren't around." *You were off with your woman.* "They'd said when I was at their property that they'd see me when they came to visit—I thought it would look more suspicious if I were rude and turned them away, told them they could just fend for themselves here. And they're nice people. As for Declan, he's just run into me a couple of times." I don't know where Paul's seen us—it has only been those few times—probably at the cafe, but maybe this was triggered by his recent evening turn-up on my doorstep. "He'd been looking out for me because he wanted to apologize for pretending to be someone else." I take a breath. "I said to you that as far as anyone would know, we'd always been just neighbours, and that's how I've kept it. You can ask your parents, if you can work out how to. Or call Declan." Work out how to ask whether they know you fucked me or whether they're oblivious. There was the incident with the photos, but that was accidental, and I don't think his mother could conclude anything definite. "I kept my word."

As I've talked the wind goes from his sails. He's quiet for a moment. "Okay. Sorry. Maybe I jumped to conclusions, and I shouldn't have blamed—" I can tell he's looking at me, but I'm looking at my front gate. "I know it wasn't all you. I was just confused, and lonely I guess, and what happened—"

It's funny how you develop an argument style growing up and stick to it. When I'm arguing I don't yell, just sound more sharply rational. I'm still doing that, but now I'm so angry. So, so angry. "You have enough women throwing themselves at you that you didn't need to rugby tackle anyone to help with your loneliness. Didn't need to tackle me." It's the remaking of history that gets to me. Trent did it, revised it all so he'd been drunk every time in his version, even though he hadn't. "I can't listen to you explaining everything away. I can't listen to any more fucking words from you." I imagine shoving him by the shoulder, pushing him into the gate, hard. "I can't." I don't want to touch him, but I do push him out the door. Not into the gate as I've imagined, just past the threshold. "Howie's upstairs and will be wondering what's going on. I need to go and lie to him now." And I close the door.

I go through the TV room, and Howie's sitting at the bend of the stairs, standing when he sees me. "Everything okay?"

He probably couldn't hear the actual conversation. "No. But please don't ask me about it right now. I'd be grateful if you didn't." He puts his hand on my shoulder as I go past him to my room.

CHAPTER 15

TWO WEEKS go by and I don't see Paul, which isn't unusual now, hasn't been for weeks. But he's actually home more now, judging by the lights in the house. And then I'm walking home from the train station and I see him on the roof. Shirtless. He looks the way he did that time—I remember laughing about it with him, remember...—what the fuck is he doing?

He looks up as I'm approaching my house, makes eye contact; I just open my door and go inside.

I sit at my desk, open my e-mail to finish up what I hadn't completed at work; sit there without typing. It's not even summer anymore, although still warm enough that he wouldn't be cold. He was sweating, so I guess he'd been working there for a while, and maybe he was really just hot. Maybe he's no longer paranoid, is finally convinced that I act towards him as towards a neighbour and nothing more, and that that's all the world sees too. Maybe he doesn't remember the joking about the shirtless roofing, has managed to forget it along with much else. But if he's just being a pricktease—the anger comes back in a flood, the way I felt when he last came knocking at my door.

I still haven't typed a single word, when Jessie pulls up outside. When she gets out of her car she starts talking, looking upwards. Paul must still be on the roof. I don't want to hear what they talk about, so I go and lie down on my bed and put on some music. Guy Sebastian sings to me of forgetting, of waking up with amnesia.

This is pathetic. As bad as a teenager, having my equilibrium disturbed this easily. I have to do something about it.

SATURDAY MORNING I visit a real estate agent. The receptionist gets me a coffee while I'm waiting. The coffee's decent: it's the kind of agency where they probably send the receptionist to barista training. There's a small plate of petits fours too. I have a token one.

"Hi, I'm Karen." She's tall and blonde and well-dressed. "Please come through."

"Thanks."

"Have a seat. You know, we're very pleased you've come to us. We've been looking for properties in your area—not just us, in fact—and none of the agencies have been having much luck."

I guess it's necessary to start off by hyping it a bit, but maybe it's true. There don't seem to have been many properties sold near me recently. Karen goes on to lay out some of the data, which reassures me she's more than just hype.

"I haven't definitely decided to sell yet; just exploring my options. It's more of a feeling that it's time to try somewhere new to live."

"Of course, we understand. We're not about the high-pressure approach at all." That was what the online reviews had said, and the reason I came here. "But if you do want to, it's a good time."

It turns out I'll almost certainly do okay if I sell. I was prepared to find out I'd make a loss and had started considering what size of loss I could bear to start afresh somewhere else. But that's not an issue, apparently. Karen gets going on her sales pitch. I'll have to think about it, and then break it to Howie. I hope he's not annoyed at making two moves in a short period of time. Maybe, if I'm lucky, he'll want to move with me.

IT'S SEVERAL days later when Paul's on the roof again. This time it's on the back roof, which I can see through my window that looks over his backyard. He's shirtless again, in the same football shorts; the toolbelt drags them down a little, exposing the jut of a hip bone. The day's cooler than the last one, and he's only just climbed onto the roof, which pushes the weight of evidence towards pricktease. I close the blinds and go into my room.

It's not much later when I hear a loud bang. Paul's dropped something off the roof? And then I hear Sam screaming, screaming and not stopping. I rush down the stairs and look over the back fence, and Paul's lying on the ground. He's not conscious. Or worse.

"Sam," I say. "Sam."

She looks up.

"I'm coming through. It's okay." I hope. I grab my phone from the kitchen bench and then go through the gate in the back fence.

I know that it's hard to find a pulse in someone else when your own heart is racing, and you fumble around, but I wait a few seconds and try a second time with his wrist, and his pulse is there. "Okay, Sam, he's just knocked out." I know there's no "just" about being knocked out, but it seems like the right thing to say. "We'll call for an ambulance, so the doctors can check your dad out." It doesn't seem like a good sign that he didn't react to Sam's screaming, but what do I know? Although I do know not to mention that.

I call the ambulance, which should be about ten minutes away.

It's only seven minutes—the hospital is close—but he's still not awake. I think that's a long time. As the paramedics put him on the gurney, he stirs, but still doesn't come to.

"We'll go in my car, okay?" I say to Sam.

She just nods.

AT THE hospital I go to the reception to find out what's happening, and to fill in whatever information they need. I've collected Paul's wallet and keys from the house—he still keeps them in a bowl in the TV room—and locked up before coming here.

"Who are you?" the reception nurse in Emergency asks when I inquire about Paul.

"His neighbour. This is his daughter, Sam." I lift her up so the nurse can see her. "Plus I have all his details here."

"Next of kin?"

"Apart from Sam here, there's an ex-wife, but I don't have her details." I guess I could get them from Declan, but I'm not sure if that will complicate things. "His parents live in Queensland, and his siblings are interstate too." Depending on what the doctor says, I'm planning to call Jack and Barb.

"Okay. It sounds like you can fill in some of this form here."

After doing that, while we wait, I let Sam play a game on my phone, which has the desired hypnotic effect. Then I think I should find out about concussion so I can anticipate what might need to be done next—specifically, whether I might need to do anything—so I take my phone back and do a quick google, and then suggest a walk to Sam to keep her occupied, exploring the hospital. I read while we're walking, half listening to Sam as she exclaims at wheelchairs and oxygen bottles.

When we get back to the waiting room the nurse says Sam can go in; she'll let me go in too, but only because she couldn't have a five-year-old wandering around the hospital by herself, it seems.

Paul's conscious but his gaze seems a bit vague. He's reclining, with the head of the bed tilted up a little. Paler than usual.

"Daddy!"

"Sammy-Sam," he says, raising himself up. As he lifts himself, he makes a sound like he's going to vomit, although he doesn't. From what I read, that's not a good sign. Not necessarily bad, but probably means they need to check further. "Aaron," he says.

"Hi."

A nurse comes past at this point. "A doctor will be along shortly."

"Can I go then?" Paul asks.

"We'll see what the doctor says."

When the nurse has gone, I say, "I didn't think to bring your phone. Sorry. I guess you might want to make some calls. I can go get it."

He looks at me with his eyebrows slightly raised. "That's okay. Thanks for bringing Sam." She's holding on to his left hand. "Kaylee isn't in Sydney at the moment, so there's no point calling her. I think I'll avoid telling her about this anyway."

"Okay." He doesn't mention Jessie, and I don't either. "Hey, Sam, will you come with me to get the phone? Maybe we can get a milkshake for you to have as well while we're waiting for the doctor." She brightens.

The round-trip to retrieve the phone and purchase the milkshake takes only twenty-five minutes. When we go back in, the doctor's just arrived and is asking Paul questions: what's his name, what's his date of birth, who's the Prime Minister. He's a bit slow on the last one, but with the rapid turnover of the last few years, that's not surprising.

"And how did this happen?"

"Uh, I'm not sure."

The doctor just waits. I know that short-term memory loss, of the minutes just before unconsciousness, isn't uncommon. The doctor prompts again. Paul still doesn't know.

"He was on the roof," I say.

"The paramedics also noticed a swelling of your right ankle. Perhaps you slipped." It might have been on the ladder—I'd imagine falling from the roof would have meant worse injuries.

"Maybe."

"Well, we'll need to do some more tests and keep you in overnight for observation."

"I have a five-year-old," Paul objects, pointing to Sam. "I can't stay overnight." He tries to sit up and makes the vomit sound again.

"I'll stay with Sam, and get her ready for school tomorrow," I say.

"I can't ask you to do that," Paul says.

"You're not asking me. I just said I'll do it." I look at him. "Unless you have some other plan to have Sam looked after."

"No," he says.

BACK AT Paul's house, I call his mother.

"Hi, Barb, it's Aaron here. Paul's neighbour."

"Aaron! This is a surprise."

"Mmm. Have you heard from Paul?" He might have called her after we left, although I'm guessing he hasn't.

"No, why?"

"There's been a bit of an accident. He slipped off a ladder, probably, and knocked himself out. He's conscious again, but the hospital's keeping him in for the night. And from what I've been reading, there might be some side effects over the next few weeks. I just thought you might want to know."

There's silence at the other end. "Thanks for letting me know. What's happening with Sam?"

"I'm going to stay with her tonight. We'll see what the doctor has to say tomorrow."

"I'll fly down."

I was kind of hoping she'd say that. "Sounds like a good idea. Apparently it can take a while to get back on your feet, although some people are back to normal straight away. It might be hard for Paul with his work as well as Sam, though." It's not unusual to only be able to work a couple of hours a day after this has happened, says my trusty source document from the US Department of Veterans Affairs.

"I should see you tomorrow, then."

"Okay. Sorry to be the bearer of bad news."

"It's still nice to hear from you."

"When will Dad come home?"

I'm chopping up an onion and some green beans I've retrieved from my place. There's a heap of pasta and sauce in the pantry. "Tomorrow." I expect that's fairly likely, but I doubt explaining probabilistic nuance to a five-year-old will help.

"How will I get to school?"

"I'll take you. I'll make you lunch in the morning, and you can tell me what else you normally need."

"There's fruit break too."

"Is an apple okay for that?"

"Yeah, I like apples." Lucky I have some at home.

Dinner's fairly quiet. I run a bath for her—she can wash herself—and after that suggest that, even though it's not the normal routine, we could watch an episode of *Xena*, and then read a book I bought her when we visited a bookshop together, all those weeks ago, one about a crocodile that gets raised as a duck. She's happy with that.

She's pretty sleepy at the end of it all. "I'll be sleeping here," I say to her. She nods.

I go and sit in the lounge room, feeling awkward. There's nowhere I can go in the house where I won't feel awkward. I think about where I'll sleep—definitely not in Paul's bed. Not on the sofa either. After Sam's gone to sleep, I'll go back to my place to get a doona and pillow, and then sleep on the floor. In the meantime, I'll find something mindless on TV.

I watch a couple of repeat episodes of a cop show, and when I look in on her, Sam's asleep. When I go back to my place Howie's there, and I give him a summary of what's happened. Then I return to Paul's, fold my doona up in front of the TV to lie on, and continue watching more of the cop show, part of what appears to be a TV marathon. I drift off eventually.

I MAKE sure to wake up a couple of hours early the next morning in case something goes wrong, but nothing does. I walk Sam to school, and get her to show me where her classroom is.

"I'll meet you here when school's finished, okay?"

"Okay."

She drops her bag, and then runs over to a group of kids who appear to be her friends. On the way out, I check with the front office what time school gets out.

After that I call in to work to take a personal leave day, and then go for a coffee, and then a second one, chatting with Axel when the cafe isn't busy.

Barb calls me to tell me that she had a friend fly her from Emerald to Brisbane, and is catching a regular flight from there. I tell her I'll pick her up. When I get to the airport, I get a call from the hospital letting me know that Paul's ready to go home. I still have his keys, too, so I think about how to schedule everything; I tell the hospital I'll come to get him.

Barb doesn't have any checked luggage, just the largest possible hand luggage, so we leave straight away. I can't really tell her any more about what happened, but I do give her a copy of the DVA fact sheet I'd printed out for her, so she can get an idea of how things might unfold over the next week or two. Dizziness, tiredness, headaches, nausea, that inability to work for longer than a couple of hours at a stretch; more. She's reading that in the car, and when she looks up we're at the hospital.

"Okay," I say. "It's also coming up to the end of school, and I told Sam I'd pick her up. And I don't think you know where her classroom is." Barb shakes her head. "So I'll leave my car with you, and you can take Paul home, and I'll walk to the school and collect Sam." I give her my keys.

"I'll try not to crash your car," she says.

"It's a lot easier to drive than that ute on your property. No column shift."

She smiles.

Collecting Sam from school is problem-free, and she's happy when I tell her that her nan is here and is picking up her dad. "You might feel like jumping on him," I say, "but he probably still has a sore head, so be gentle."

"I can be gentle," she says. Perhaps she can, although it'll be quite uncharacteristic.

Inside, Paul's sitting on the sofa. From the sounds coming from the direction of the kitchen, Barb's out there.

"Daddy!" shouts Sam. She runs towards him, but slows down at the last moment, and inches forward for a hug, arms outstretched.

"Watch out for my foot," he says. "It turns out I've sprained my ankle. It's not broken, fortunately." I see it's bandaged up, though.

"I'm going to get a drink," says Sam, and she goes out to the kitchen.

As soon as she goes, a vertical crease appears between Paul's eyebrows. "Why did you call my mum?"

I shrug. "I made an executive decision." I toss a second copy of the DVA fact sheet onto the sofa next to him. The fact sheet also mentions that irritability is a typical symptom, but only in the sense that the chance of someone with concussion being irritable is higher than usual. That doesn't help work out whether a particular instance of irritation is due to the injury or just regular annoyance. I decide to be charitable and assume it's the injury. "The effects might take a while to wear off, according to this," I continue, indicating the sheet. "Obviously, you can get straight back into everything, but apparently that can cause more problems if you don't take it easier at first, start with a couple of days' rest. I'm sure the doctor's told you all of this anyway."

The crease smooths out. "Yeah, I guess that's sensible. Anyway, thanks for looking after Sam."

"No problem at all."

He hesitates. "Any suggestions for something to read while I'm resting up?"

"No." While irritability, fatigue, and anxiety are apparently symptoms, a desire to jerk your neighbour around is not, so I don't have to charitably attribute this to the injury. My books and Greek stories and all that bullshit, as he called it—that's just for me now.

I go into the kitchen. "I'll be heading off now," I say to Barb and Sam.

"You won't stay?" says Barb.

"'Fraid not. I'm sure I'll see you again while you're here, though."

"What about the other part of that *Xena* episode?" asks Sam. Last night was the first half of a two-parter.

"Another time. Go hang out with your dad. You can tell him about school today."

IT'S ONLY an hour later when there's a knock on my door. It's Paul.

"Hello," I say.

"Mum asked if you'd like to have dinner with us. She's cooking. Said you'll have to eat anyway."

166

I look at him. He's still pale. "Come on," I say, "that'd just be awkward. Tell your mum there's something I have to do and that I can't make it. A Skype call for work."

"What if I want you to come too?"

"I'd say that you're just feeling confused and lonely, and think I look like a likely sucker." I didn't mean to say that last part; it made its way past my rational argument filter. "Sorry. But you'll get better soon, get over this feeling. I don't get over things in quite the same way." I shouldn't have said that last part either. "Just go home and get some rest."

That was a bit harsh, I think, as he hobbles down my front steps, slightly slumped at the shoulders. But necessary.

After that I go up to my room. Guy Sebastian sings to me again, telling me that whoever said that it's better to have loved and lost than to have never loved at all, they were wrong. They were wrong.

CHAPTER 16

SATURDAY IS a day for just hanging around the house with Howie. We've decided to do a *Game of Thrones* marathon. I'm behind—haven't finished the third season—but Howie hasn't seen any of it at all, and wants to find out what it's all about, so we start from the beginning, each lying on a sofa.

After the first episode of the first season:

"Oh my God! They pushed ten-year-old Bran out of the window! And it's all incesty."

"That sets the tone for the whole show, really."

After the third episode:

"Did you know that Sveta has broken up with Ted?" Howie asks.

"Yeah."

"I only just found out."

"I haven't known for that long."

"I think Ted was sneaking around behind her back. A bit tame compared to *Game of Thrones* drama, but still scummy."

"So how do you feel about Sveta being single?"

"It's too soon to do anything, I think. But you know, I do like her. If you and I hadn't talked before, I would have just gone along with my friend-zone glasses on. You know, the way you get to seeing someone without really seeing them because you're so used to them. It was kind of like I got to take them off, and see Sveta again the way I first saw her. She's pretty hot, really."

"Yeah, you're not the only guy who thinks so. So it's a good idea to take your time, but don't take forever."

"Fair enough."

After the seventh episode:

168

"So have you thought more about how you feel about me moving house?" I ask. "Would you come? We could do a TV show binge like this whenever you like."

"Yeah, I've been thinking about it. I like it here, but I'm okay with moving again. Don't make a habit of it, though."

"I figure I'll rent for six months while I look around for another house to buy. So it's like an extra six months' probation, to make sure I'm still fulfilling the requirements for a decent housemate."

"I haven't asked, but is selling the house connected with—"

"Yes."

"That's kind of major."

"Yeah. But a fresh start is a good thing."

After the tenth and final episode:

"Who's your favourite character in this season of *Game of Thrones*?" Howie asks.

"Give me a couple of minutes to think. You go first, since you asked."

"Daenerys." The Mother of Dragons. Of course. She's both thoroughly likeable—a bit of a rarity in the show—and tough. And hot.

"Of course. My favourite's either Tyrion or Varys. This season, probably Varys."

"The eunuch? That's a weird choice."

"I wouldn't go in for the whole physical aspect. But he's in control." He's rational and powerful, the master of the spy network and the knowledge that comes with it. And he's one of the few characters whose life isn't messed up by love.

I've recently been wondering—been worrying, mildly at least—whether the strength of my feelings about Paul might represent some psychological issue. That the unrequitedness of them, for someone who just wants to be straight, might represent a kind of subconscious self-sabotage, after Trent. It's true my other major relationships weren't like this. Leo got a great opportunity at a graphic design studio in the US, and although he met someone over there in the months when I was trying to sort out a visa, it wasn't unexpected, and it didn't feel like the end of the world. Crazy Gunther was only ever going to be an extended holiday romance. Alexander and I grew apart over the year we lived together after a year going out before that, stopped doing things together, even when I'd try to find things we might want to do; I still don't know precisely why it ended—probably me.

There's no rational reason I've felt so strongly about Paul. Leo and Alexander and even Gunther were much more suitable boyfriends.

Maybe I should go and see someone. Get myself fixed. Not fixed like Varys, though. In the meantime, I think the practical steps are helping. Keeping myself busy, moving house.

I'm in control.

I FIGURE I should tell Paul I'm moving, so the next day I knock on his door.

It takes a while, but he eventually answers it. "Hi."

"Hi. I was wondering how you were doing."

"Okay, thanks. I'm back to working mornings and afternoons now, with a short nap around lunchtime. I tried a whole day of work without a break a few days ago, took on three fairly big jobs, and had a massive headache by night-time, so I've slowed up a bit again. I guess medical advice is useful." He smiles. "Thanks again for all your help."

"That's sounding good." I'm not sure how to segue. "Something else—I'm selling the house. I just thought I'd tell you before the For Sale sign goes up next weekend. There'll be inspections, people in and out."

"Err." He seems lost for words. "Is it to do with—?"

"Yeah. But that's okay. Things happen."

He looks like he's groping for the right thing to say, and there's silence until he comes out with, "I was just opening a beer out the back when you knocked. Mum and Sam have just gone to the park. Do you want to come in and have one too?"

"No." I don't want to sit out in his backyard drinking beer and remembering the other times we've done that there, the other things we've done there. But I'm in control, moving on—and away—so I don't have to be hard-hearted. "We can get a coffee if you like."

He hesitates.

"We don't have to." I start to turn away.

"Yeah, let's do that."

He closes the door behind him, and we walk to the cafe. He's only limping very slightly now. I realize I'd forgotten the smell of him; not forgotten, but not registered its absence.

"Do you know where you're moving?"

"Not yet. I'll rent somewhere for a while before I buy again."

He nods, but doesn't have much more to say before we arrive.

Axel's there as usual and says hello. Paul heads to the back of the cafe, where there aren't many people, and chooses a table near the kitchen and the toilets. The most out-of-the-way table, one for having a serious conversation at, perhaps. Or one to avoid being seen at.

"Long black for you?" Axel asks me.

"Yep."

"For me too," says Paul. Then, when Axel leaves with the order, he continues, "I'm not sure how to say what I want to say. Maybe I'll start by saying that I feel bad that you're moving because of me."

I shrug. "As I said, stuff happens."

"I'm sorry about the things I said. I wish I could take them back, fix things between us."

I shrug again. "You want a regular life. I understand that. I just can't watch you have it. It's pretty painful."

"I thought you'd just kind of flicked a switch, stopped liking me. Understandably. You didn't seem angry when I broke things off. Just like, okay, that's the end of that. It was only that last conversation where I thought, I guess it did matter."

"Of course I was upset." I pause. "I guess we argue differently. To me, the way you argue, like with Kaylee, feels pretty vicious. My way probably seems cold to you. But, you know, I don't just casually tell people I love them." I don't look at him when I say that. That's too intense. But I'll be leaving soon. "Anyway, it doesn't matter. You have your life, with Jessie, and I'll have my separate life."

That's the point at which Axel brings the coffee. We're silent until he leaves again.

Paul takes a sip and makes a face. "That's bitter."

I sip mine: it's just as I like it. "Perfect for me, then." I smile to be clear it's a joke, although it's a little bit true.

"Actually, my life doesn't have Jessie," Paul continues. "We broke up."

"Sorry. But maybe it's just your traumatic brain injury." That's how the fact sheet talks about it, even for mild cases. "Irritation, impulsive decisions—they're to be expected. You might patch things up."

"We broke up before that." He pauses. This is a conversation with a lot of pauses. "I had this dumb idea, and breaking up with her was how I started it off. You'd made it clear you didn't want to talk, so I thought—well, maybe the shirtless trick will work." That shirtless day on the front roof, and then the one on the back roof, the day he fell off and went to hospital.

"Jesus! You're lucky I didn't smack you one for that."

"I said it was dumb. I suppose I hoped we'd just fall into doing stuff and things would work out."

"Jesus, Mary, and Joseph, do you think I'm like some puppy that's just waiting for you to whistle?"

"No! No. I just hoped you might think, hey, he's still interested and wants something to happen. Dumb, dumb, dumb."

"Even if you wanted something to happen, just to patch things up, the prospect of another episode of it-was-never-really-real is a sticking point for me. I've been through it all before—before you— and that time was enough. The it-didn't-really-happen, the maybe-it-did-happen-but-I-was-confused, the okay-it-happened-but-no-one-saw-it. The Bart Simpson sequence of denials."

"I didn't—okay, I did. I know I said I was confused. But I know it all happened, and that sometimes it was me that made it happen. When I tackled you at that footie game in the park. When we had sex that first time after I fell on you on the couch." He starts fidgeting. "When I gave you a blow job. When I—when I did you, at the end of that day we spent at the beach; I can't get that out of my head. When you gave me a blow job by the waterhole in Emerald. When you gave me a blow job in my backyard. That last one, I was getting ready to relive it when you came by this morning."

Well, that's not denial. I swallow. I'm getting hard, a bit. More than a bit. "Okay. But it's not just the sex. It was a lot more than that for me. And who's to say you're not just being driven by your hormones at the moment?"

"I have more to say. But I, uh, I'll be back in a minute."

He gets up from behind the table. His shorts are tented way out; his cock is almost fully hard, pointing down and to the left; the head of it is poking out of the leg. I guess the reliving of the backyard blow job included not wearing underpants. He tries to adjust himself, but his cock slips back to where it was; he hunches slightly and goes quickly to the toilet.

This back half of the cafe is still almost empty of patrons, and those who are there are engaged in their own conversations. However, it's not empty of Axel, who's making for the kitchen. He comes over and grins.

"Can I get you some more coffee?" We've both finished.

"Two more again. And after that, can you make yourself scarce?"

His grin gets wider. "Of course. You know, in such a public place here, I never would have suspected—"

"There's nothing to suspect. Go away."

"I saw what there was to suspect. But I'll go away."

"Thanks. It's kind of serious, in spite of what you think you saw."

"Well, all the best, then." And he finally goes away, taking his grin with him.

It's some time before Paul comes back, and the coffees have arrived before he does. His shorts are noticeably fuller than usual, but he's no longer at risk of an indecent exposure arrest. He sees the coffee and grimaces slightly. "I'm going to put some sugar in this time."

He picks up where he left off. "Now my hormones have nothing to do with what I'm saying." I visualize him jerking off in the bathroom, then waiting until he looked respectable again. "So I also miss hanging out with you, and having you come over, and reading books with you, and talking about stuff."

"Friend stuff."

"Well, sort of, but I want it all the time. Not just the occasional catch-up." I could do the occasional catch-up once I move, if we were going to be just friends. Not more. Maybe some time in the distant future it could be more like the friendship I have with Howie and Sveta, but I can't visualize that. "Plus I already mentioned the sex. It's more than just friend stuff."

Maybe he does want more. It's a huge risk. "Maybe this is part of the after-effects of your brain being knocked about. Feeling a bit depressed, maybe manifested as loneliness, could explain it." Sometimes I sound like an android even to myself.

He's frowning slightly. "You know, what you were saying about explaining things away—you do it too. Is there anything I can say that you couldn't explain away by hormones or a bang on the head or whatever?"

That's true, and I hadn't really thought of that before. And more: he's having an argument, but not with that tight-voiced anger. It's my argument style. Such a strange thing to be the decisive factor in changing my mind.

"Fair point. But it's still possible, and you might feel differently tomorrow or next week. So how about we just see how things go. Try to be normal in the meantime."

His smile's a broad one.

THE NEXT day after I get home from work, Barb drops in. I'm still in work trousers and shirt, although I've loosened the collar.

"I just wanted to let you know I'm heading home at the end of the week."

"I guess that means Paul's pretty much better. Sorry I haven't seen you much while you've been here."

"I suppose you've been busy."

"Yeah, work."

She just looks at me.

"Err, would you like to come in for a cuppa?"

"Yes, thanks."

We go through to the kitchen, and Gabi comes to wind her way around my legs. Barb squats down to pat her, with a slight wince as her knee clicks audibly. Once I've made the tea, we sit on the stools at the kitchen bench.

"You won't guess who I met down here," she says. "It's a funny small world." I do guess. "It's Declan, Paul's ex-brother-in-law. I knew he'd moved to Sydney, but had no idea it was around here. We just ran into him in the park, Sam and I. And it turns out he knows you, even though he hasn't been in contact with Paul down here. Isn't that funny?"

"Funny," I echo.

"He had a lot to say about you. All good things. He's a nice boy. It was a shame he had a hard time in Emerald. He used to come over a lot with his sister. Often helped me make dinner. Peeled the potatoes, cut up the beans." She purses her lips and blows on the tea, looking at me. I notice for the first time that, although Paul looks so much like his father, his eyes have the shape and colour of hers, that sharp light blue. The steam rises from her mug; it's like a physical manifestation of the silence that's suddenly looming up between us. It wasn't just the photos on my phone that were the giveaway.

"Yeah, Declan's a nice guy. I think he felt like a bit of an outsider in Emerald. I got that impression too when I went to the O'Connells' that night before I left."

"Yes," she says, "that was a shame, him feeling he had to leave. He does seem to have settled in well here at least. Like you. Like Paul could. Anyway, I was going to ask if you could look in on Paul occasionally after I'm gone. I'm sure he'd appreciate it."

I nod.

CHAPTER 17

I SHIFT my work routine. Instead of working until late, I get up two hours earlier and go to the gym before it's light, and then get into the office before most people have arrived. Dean, when he comes around for a morning coffee, is surprised that I'm not still just taking care of e-mail, but have been coding up some improved random number generation algorithms and testing them out.

When I get home it's early, and I knock on Paul's door and go in. They're having dinner, as I knew they would be.

"Hi, Aaron!" says Sam. "Do you want to play with my Lego after dinner?"

"Hi," says Paul. He looks a bit surprised. Not in a bad way, I think.

"Would you like to join us?" says Barb. "Paul cooked tonight, and he's always making too much."

"Sure, that'd be great."

"I'll get another chair," says Paul. He comes back with one of the plastic ones from outside, and a beer.

THE NEXT day Paul comes over after Sam's gone to bed. "Would you like to go out on Friday? Mum has said she'll mind Sam."

"Go out?"

"Yeah. Like a date. I mean, it would be an actual date."

"Okay."

"How about I pick you up at seven o'clock?"

"You'll pick me up?" I'm not meaning to be difficult—it feels like any misstep could collapse it all again—but these questions just come out of my mouth.

"Isn't that what you say on dates? I've never really done them. I'm going by TV shows."

"It's just that we're neighbours and I don't need picking up. But sure. I'll expect you on my doorstep at seven." Jesus. Just a *Yes* right at the start would have been so much smoother.

PAUL HAS a new wardrobe. Or at least one new outfit. It's not his blue-on-blue; it's more like something he could have found in Howie's wardrobe, or mine. A metrosexual-or-maybe-gay look. He's hot, still, but it's different.

"So I thought we could go and see this movie, and then have dinner, eh." He still sounds like himself. "What do you reckon?"

"Sounds good. What's the movie?"

"You'll see when we get there. It's just at the local cinema." The cinema's an independent one and shows a mix of the latest big-budget releases, foreign films, and wacky-with-the-occasional-gem indie productions.

It turns out we're going indie. "I found out about it on the Internet," he says. From the poster that's stuck up in an obscure corner at the back of the cinema waiting area, the cast appears to include two drag queens, a gay couple into S&M, and half a dozen twinks. I think he must have typed the query "gayest gay GAY movie" into Google.

It's not one of the gems, but it's not totally painful. I spend almost as much time sneaking looks at Paul as I do watching the movie. It's nice of him to do this.

After the movie he asks, "Any preference for dinner?" He's smiling fairly fixedly.

"Thai?"

"Sure." There are a few relatively cheap places close by, but we walk past them and go somewhere a bit fancier. It's busy, and the polished wood makes it echoey, but it's pretty good: I've been here before. We're seated by a Thai waiter.

"So, err, the movie," says Paul.

"I appreciate that you went to the trouble of finding out about movies on the Internet."

He lets out a sigh. "I reckon that's a polite slam of my choice. Which is kind of a relief because I didn't know if I was supposed to like it."

I laugh. "You don't have to like it. You don't have to anything. Just be your normal self." Maybe leaving out any part that still wants to be straight, at least while you're on a date with me. "You don't have to dress differently either. Although you do look hot in that shirt."

"Really?" he says. "I thought I might look like a wanker. How about this, then?" He undoes the next top button and makes a fake-sexy look, eyelids drooping and lips pouting. It reminds me of Howie's pretend Zoolander face. Then he reverts to his normal expression. "Uh, I'm not whistling to you or anything."

I laugh. "No, really, you look good. Although maybe this would be over the top." I reach across the table and undo another button, pull the top of his shirt apart to show more of his chest. I mean it as a joke, but suddenly it doesn't feel like one to me. Time to step back.

That's when a waiter comes over to take our order. We quickly look at our menus again.

EARLY NEXT morning Paul and Sam take Barb to the airport, and I wave them off from my front steps. When they get back, Kaylee comes to pick up Sam for the week.

Last night was pretty good. I mean, the movie wasn't great, and Paul went a bit overboard in trying to be cool with gay stuff, but it was definitely one of those times when the cliché is true, that it's the thought that counts. I just went back to my house after dinner, by myself, but the parting at our front gates wasn't awkward.

Today I'm feeling the tiniest bit of hope.

I'm in the park, skyping on my laptop with Deelie. She's thinking about a major art project she has to do this year, and is still at the stage of considering options.

"How about a painting, pre-Raphaelite, of the three original *Star Wars* main characters? Leia with her hair down out of the buns, floating over her shoulders while the light of twin suns shines on her and she looks soulfully into the distance. Whatever."

"Ugh, your ideas are so dumb."

I glance up, and see Paul walking through the park, wearing his cowboy hat tilted back on his head. The hat I bought in Emerald, along with the shorts I borrowed there and never had the opportunity to return, are in a box in the storage space at the top of my wardrobe, covered, so I don't accidentally see them and get reminded. I'm reminded now. Paul looks across at me and hesitates. I hesitate too, and then beckon him over. He comes and sits next to me, cross-legged on the grass.

"Paul, this is my sister, Cordelia. Deelie, Paul, my neighbour."

"Ah. Are you Sam's dad?"

"Yep, that's me."

"We're not talking about anything important," I say. "Well, it's Deelie's art project at school for this year, which is important, but it's still undecided what it will be. It's just unimportant ideas we've been bouncing around." I expect her to say something to the effect that the ideas are stupid rather than unimportant, but she doesn't. She's looking at Paul through the webcam.

Paul notices too. "Do I have something on my face? Oil?" He wipes at his chin and his cheeks.

"No," says Deelie, "I could just see you in a Bunny painting. The hat, your face. Like a modern version of the style. That could be cool."

"That's Rupert Bunny the artist she's talking about," I say. "Nothing about rabbits. Maybe you could do a picture of him like the one with Cthulhu rising out the water behind the guy."

"Who's Cthulhu?" asks Paul.

"A creepy old monster god," says Deelie. "Aaron used to read me some of those stories when I was younger. If you want to read any of them—I don't know why you would, but anyway—Aaron will definitely be able to suggest a book."

"Maybe he will, one day."

Hmm.

"It wasn't actually Cthulhu, just some sea monster," I say. "If you wanted it to be all Australian, maybe you could have a giant platypus rising out of the water behind him, with snakes coming out of its shoulders like tentacles."

"Yeah, sure," she says, scornfully dismissive. "Or paint him at a creek, with a giant echidna with snakes for spines looming behind?"

"A giant tiger snake," suggests Paul, "with snakes coming out of its—not-shoulders?"

It gets sillier after that.

I SPEND most of the afternoon—which is storming, after a morning of bright sunshine—reading a history of Mycenaean Greece while Howie watches the tennis on TV. When I go up to my room just after sunset, to put away some washing, I notice out the window that Paul's backyard light is on. I notice he's sitting in a chair in the backyard. I notice that he's naked, and his shorts are next to the chair, and he's hard and stroking himself. I can see his abs tense, arrhythmically, as if he's close; he stops stroking; touches himself again; stops: he's edging. He looks up directly at my window—I'm sure he sees me—looks away again. His abs tense again.

"What's going on?"

I whirl around. Howie's coming up the stairs. I fumble with the blind, lower it.

"Nothing."

"What?"

"Nothing." I laugh. "Nothing to see here. Move along."

He looks at me doubtfully, then shrugs. "Okay." He keeps going up the stairs, but as he passes the window, he lunges for the blind. I anticipate him—we've known each other a long time, after all—I'm laughing so hard I almost miss intercepting him, but I push him up the stairs.

"Just go and do whatever you were going to do."

He does—I wait a minute to see if he's going to rush back down the stairs—and then I peek out the blind. Paul's gone. I pull the blind back up.

A few minutes later, Howie goes past my room as I'm folding clothes. "What was that all about?"

I can't help laughing. "Nothing. Have you looked out the window? Nothing there, right?"

He narrows his eyes. "Hmm."

I GO to bridge, arriving fairly late on purpose. Two games are in full swing; I notice that Gray isn't there, as I expected he wouldn't be. I say hi to everyone and go through to Lance in the kitchen, kiss him hello.

He talks about the latest publishing debacle, and I wait until he pauses to check whatever's in the oven before I say, "Have you heard from Gray?"

"No, why? Is everything okay?"

"He might not come back to bridge. We were kind of seeing each other—"

"I could tell. He did moon over you a bit."

"Well. It wasn't really working out, so I broke it off. I was kind of emotionally involved with someone else, which has been a big mess—I'd thought it was over, but maybe it isn't. In any case, it's complicated everything else, including Gray."

"Was kind of emotionally involved?"

"Am."

"Is it the dishy LA fellow?"

"No. There might be more to tell, if anything ever gets resolved. I feel bad about Gray, though, because he's a nice guy."

"Well, I'd prescribe reading *The Remains of the Day* and listening to a whole lot of torch songs. Adele's albums on repeat."

"I don't think any human could do all that and maintain the will to live."

"At least read Ishiguro."

Paul's suggested going out with Howie and Sveta. To the Imperial. So I arrange it with them for Saturday.

"Your property dispute over, then?" asks Howie.

"Getting there."

The Saturday morning is the first property inspection for prospective buyers and time-rich neighbourhood gawkers. We've tidied up pretty extensively: Howie's always been good with that.

"The usual suggestions to make the place more attractive are to brew coffee and bake bread," I say. "And then to disappear. I think we should stay, though. I will make some coffee, but I'll skip making bread; instead, I thought you could look decorative. See if your cheekbones can push up the price."

Howie rolls his eyes. "I'd better get a commission, then."

He does get a bit dressed up, though, a bit preppy. Karen the agent arrives fifteen minutes before the open house starts, and seems happy with everything. Howie and I go and sit in the backyard, drink the coffee that I've made, and read the newspaper.

There's quite a bit of interest, both in the house and in Howie: he's very charming.

"Are you definitely selling?" asks Howie during a lull.

"Not sure yet. I'll see how things go."

"Things."

"Yeah, things."

When the open house is over, Karen comes out into the backyard to say she thinks it all went well, and we probably won't need any more of these sessions after the originally scheduled next two.

After that Howie gets changed for an afternoon at the beach with Sveta.

Howie's going to the Imperial from Sveta's, so I go to Paul's after having a second shower for the day and getting changed. He's wearing his new shirt, but also the boots that used to be his standard going-out ones, polished up. We walk to the Imperial together.

"So does Howie know about us?"

"I still haven't told him. But he's not dumb—he has been living with me, after all, and knows me well. I think he's probably guessed some of it."

"That's cool," says Paul.

When we get there, Sveta and Howie are both there already. They're standing close together; Howie's hand is in Sveta's back pocket.

"Hello, Paul," says Sveta. "It's been a while since I've seen you."

Howie, more tactful, says, "I heard about you falling off that ladder. How are you feeling?"

That gets a normal conversation going. As Paul's telling them about the scan the hospital did of his head, he leans into me, one shoulder just behind mine, resting against me. I see Sveta nudge Howie in the ribs; she thinks she's subtle.

When Paul excuses himself to go to the toilet, Sveta barely waits until he's out of earshot before she says to Howie, "I told you so, right from early on."

I look at them both. "I'll explain later. And apologize." To Howie: "I'd promised."

"No worries," says Howie.

"Anyway, don't get ahead of yourselves. It's all a bit tentative at the moment."

"Pfft," says Sveta. "That shoulder thing wasn't tentative."

When Paul comes back, it's all comfortable.

AT OUR front gate, Paul gives me a hug. It's definitely not a bro hug. Howie and I go into our place, and Sveta comes too: it's not the first night she's stayed over.

"You're just coming back here by yourself?" Howie asks me.

"Yes. Why do you always think I'm going to be inviting people back? I'm perfectly fine living in a sexual desert, as you called it once. Less complicated."

"Jeez, you're strange." He and Sveta head up to his room. I stay and watch TV for a short while—that way I can minimize the amount of noise I overhear from Howie's room.

On my way up the stairs, I notice Paul's backyard light on again. And he's there again, naked again, stroking again. I close the blind; consider. Then I go downstairs, quietly, and out the back door. I hadn't noticed through the window that the gate between our back fences is open, but I do now. I go through.

"Hi," I say.

"Hi," says Paul. He pauses in his stroking; swallows, his Adam's apple bobbing.

"I saw you the other night too."

"I know."

"It's a lucky coincidence that it was those two evenings when I looked out the window and saw you. And that Howie didn't."

"Actually, not coincidence. I've been out here each night. I'm not doing it to whistle you over, and I'm trying to do the normal stuff too, but I thought it wouldn't hurt to remind you I'm interested." He pauses again in his stroking, which has slowed. "Although, jeez, it feels like my dick is going to fall off after all this."

I laugh. "I hope not. I like your dick. But just to be sure it doesn't, maybe we should let it rest. For a week. Or two."

He groans. "Don't even joke about that. I'll explode."

"Go inside?" I ask.

"Yeah." I pull him up by his cock. When he's standing, I draw him close and breathe him in.

Up in his room, he gets out a packet of condoms from his bedside table, and a container of lube. He holds them up.

"You're hopeful," I say.

"I bought them on Sunday. Yeah, I'm hopeful."

He watches me get undressed. "The way you lowered yourself onto my dick that time, I loved that. I love the way your face looks when I'm inside you. I love you."

Maybe he only means it now, in the heat of it all. But maybe he means more than that. I can't live my life always explaining away anything positive.

I grip him by the shoulders and lower him onto the bed, an echo of the first time we did this, and straddle his legs. However, this time I'm not all prepared.

"So it doesn't just work without preparation," I say to him. "Not for me, anyway. Last time I did it I got myself ready in the bathroom before, and that was a while ago."

"A while ago?"

"That time with you." I almost add, *Of course*, but he's not to know. "So I have to ease myself open." I squeeze some lube on my hand and spread it around my hole. "You can put a condom on while I'm doing that." I insert my middle finger, wincing slightly at first, then sliding it back and forth. It starts feeling good pretty quickly. Paul's put on the condom and is watching me. I slide in a second finger.

"Can I do that?" asks Paul.

"You sure?"

"Yeah, I'm sure," he says in a voice with a trace of huskiness.

I shuffle up along his body—he inhales as I brush over his cock—and he slowly pushes two lubed-up fingers into me. It's more intense than when I do it to myself. I close my eyes for a moment, then open them again and look at Paul. "That's probably enough."

"Could you come from me just doing that?" He keeps sliding his fingers in and out, each time a little deeper.

"Yes. And from looking at you while you're doing it. But I don't want that." I edge back so that his fingers are forced to slip out, and reach behind me until I can feel his cock. I position it at my hole, and then push slowly back onto it.

It's as good as the first time.

AFTER, I'M lying on top of him. He says into my ear, "Just so you know, even after my hormones have been satisfied, I still love you. And I'm sorry for what I did to you. And I want us to be together. How about you?"

I kiss his jaw. "I want that. I'm not one for casual flings. I couldn't keep doing this if it was just some casual on-off thing."

Paul puts on a passable version of Scudder's West Country accent. "Then we shan't never be parted."

MAREK MORAN is, in his day job, a computer science professor. If you want to know about shortest-path graph algorithms, he's your man. However, that's probably not why you're reading this. He currently lives in Sydney, Australia, and has previously lived in France, Germany, and the US. He enjoys traveling around and listening to people talk: he's learned to respond to enquiries after his wellbeing with a ça va merci, sehr gut danke, or copacetic, thanks.

The only member of his book club to like George Eliot's *Mill on the Floss*, he's discovered that he enjoys writing romance as well as reading it; the other members of his book club don't yet know this. He plays piano, squash, and his cards close to his chest. *The Sparky* is his first novel.

He will be delighted to receive your e-mail at marekmorangie@ gmail.com.

CHASE THE ACE

CLARE LONDON

A LONDON LADS STORY

www.dreamspinnerpress.com

Also from Dreamspinner Press

FOR **MORE** OF THE **BEST GAY** ROMANCE

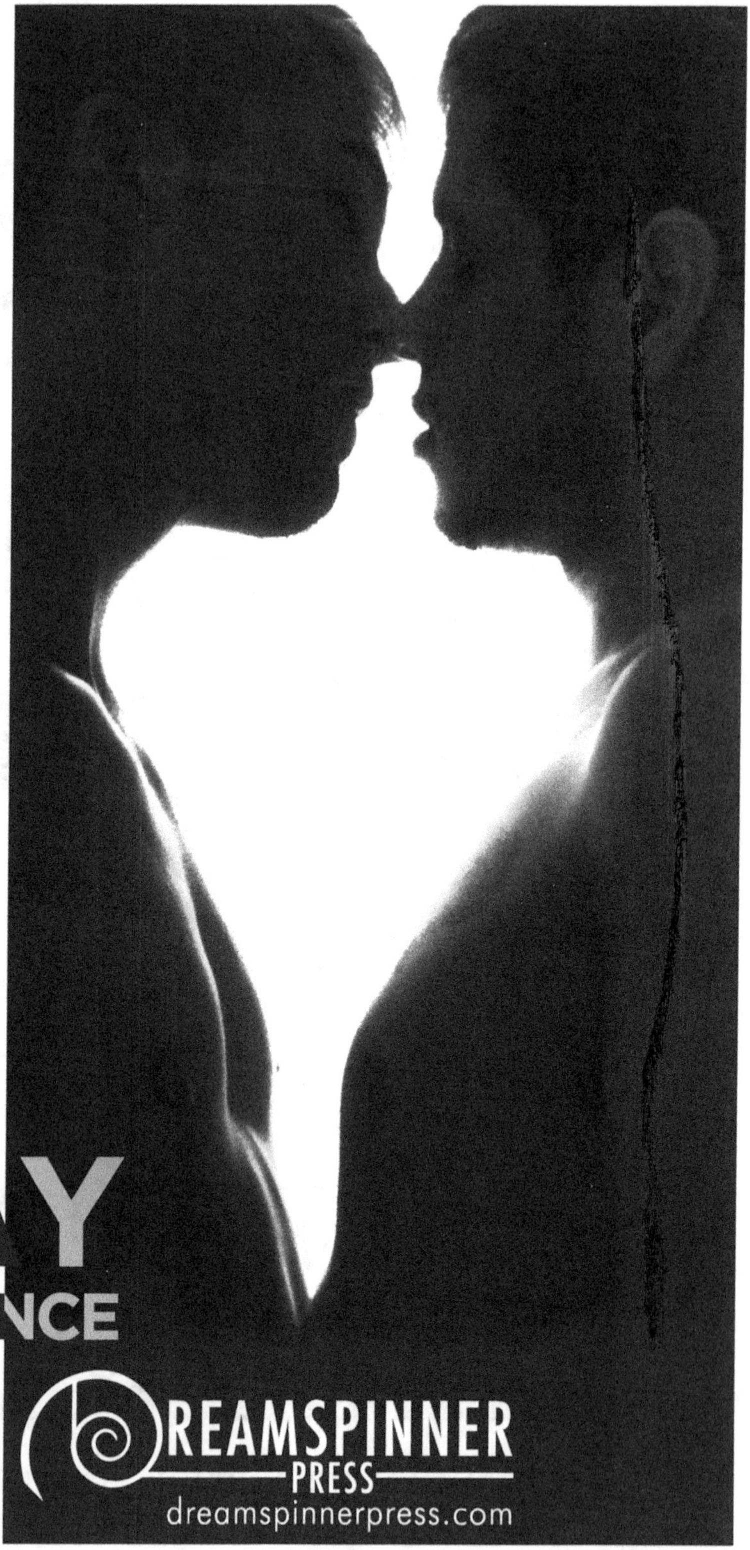

DREAMSPINNER
PRESS

dreamspinnerpress.com

www.ingramcontent.com/pod-product-compliance
Lightning Source LLC
Chambersburg PA
CBHW060103260626
47160CB00005B/1776